DEDICATION

There are those to whom I can never show this book, but who were the driving inspiration behind it.

This book is for them.

CONTENTS

ACKNOWLEDGMENTS

Published by Cassidy Storm
Edited by Candice Royer
Graphics by Allie Mitchell
.

PART ONE

THE UNKNOWN CALLER

The phone rang. Autumn checked the display: *UNKNOWN CALLER.* She pressed the green "answer" icon.

"Hello?"

A female voice greeted her. "So. You were just about to tell me how wet you are."

Autumn's jaw dropped in surprise, and she gave a little giggle. "I... *think* you've got the wrong number."

A pause.

"Are you sure about that?"

Autumn frowned. *Ok, who's fucking with me?* "Steph? Is that you?"

Even as she said it, she knew it wasn't. Her friend Stephanie was a prankster with a whacked sense of humor, sure, but Autumn had just gotten the phone that afternoon and hadn't shared the number with anyone yet.

"No, I'm definitely not Steph."

"Okay. I just got this phone today," Autumn explained. "You're probably trying to, um, reach, whoever had this number before..."

"Maybe." The caller's voice remained low, melodious. Mysterious.

"Well, look, I have a date. I've gotta go. It was nice, uh, talking to you."

A mirthful, throaty laugh. "Have fun on your *date*... Don't do anything I wouldn't do."

Shaking her head, Autumn ended the call, turning her attention back to her make-up.

Autumn willed herself not to roll her eyes as her date — *Brian? Brad?* — droned on. So far, she'd been regaled with twenty minutes of details about how great he was at his job and how rich he was going to be just as soon as the stock market did this and the Euro did that. Now he was launching into a diatribe about his car, how much the MSRP was, and how Brian-or-Brad's savvy negotiating skills had gotten *five thousand dollars!* knocked off the asking price. Autumn listened intently as Brian-or-Brad explained how *she* could and should negotiate the next time she was

4

in the market for a new Lexus.

You picked a winner this time, she admonished herself, cursing herself for not having set up a "bail-out plan." She'd gone on her share of blind dates, especially recently. Usually, she'd have one of her friends on standby to call about an "emergency" at the "office", but having just gotten her phone service back on, she hadn't had a chance to contact anyone with her new number yet.

Briefly, she considered disappearing to the ladies' room and never coming back. But she'd always considered that to be extremely classless. *Someone took time out to accept a date and buy me dinner — I can at least have the courtesy to not "ghost" him*, she reasoned.

Across the table, Brian-or-Brad was now lecturing her that when it came to purchasing a big-ticket item, such as a car or a flat-screen television, *anything* was negotiable.

Yep, those nine-fifty-an-hour sales "associates" down at my Walmart sure are shrewd negotiators.

Mercifully, the food arrived. *Great, he'll have to stop talking while he eats, at least.*

But it wasn't to be.

Brian-or-Brad was scrutinizing her plate with a critical eye. "Didn't you order medium rare?"

"Yeah."

He frowned. "That doesn't look like medium rare." Taking his butter knife, he deftly poked at the top of her steak. "Nope, it's definitely not medium rare." Immediately, he began explaining exactly how he was able to determine this, which led to a short "elevator pitch" detailing his culinary expertise on top of everything else.

"It's fine, really," she assured him, even as he had his hand up to flag down their server.

"Nonsense. My girls deserve the best."

Did he really just say "my girls"? Okay, yeah, I'm going to the bathroom and ghosting him.

But just then, her phone rang. Once again, it was an *UNKNOWN CALLER* — possibly, the same freaky one from earlier. Regarding it for a moment, she pressed the red icon to send to voicemail — then remembered she hadn't yet set it up.

"Everything okay?"

"Yeah, sorry." Autumn thought for a second and decided to take the "out" she'd been given. "Well, no. That was my sister calling. She'll be wanting to know if I can babysit." She frowned apologetically. "She said they might call her in to work..."

Autumn was surprised at how easily the lie flowed from her lips. In truth, of a family of four children, she'd been the only girl—but it didn't really make a difference, as Brian-or-Brad was never going to know that anyway.

"Do you have to go?" Her blind date looked absolutely crestfallen.

She mustered her best *jeez-this-really-sucks* expression. "Yeah. 'Fraid so."

As they waited for the check, Brian-or-Brad apparently realized he hadn't yet fascinated his date with a description of his rent-controlled loft apartment on the West Side, or the timeshare in Florida he'd have access to once he became a partner. Quickly, he attempted to cram this exciting information in, plus recaps of his successful job and his pricey Lexus.

"I'll email you?" Brian-or-Brad asked as they parted

ways outside the restaurant.

"Uh, sure." She smiled. "Thanks for dinner, Brian."

"Brad."

Oh, well, it was a 50-50 shot, she thought as she exited in a hurry.

"Netflix, it is," Autumn announced to her empty apartment. As she was searching through the couch cushions for the remote, her phone went off. *UNKNOWN* again.

"Hello?"

"So how was your date?" The warm, quietly confident voice suggested that Miss UNKNOWN already knew the answer.

"It was... okay," Autumn said cautiously.

"That good, huh?"

"Yeah. Hey, did you try to call earlier?"

"Yeah. Your mailbox wasn't set up yet. Otherwise, I

would have left you a message." A slight hint of suggestiveness on the last word. Autumn wondered just what the "message" might have been.

"Well, like I said, I just got this phone. I don't know who you're trying to reach, but this number—"

The voice was soft, very hypnotizing. "I'm trying to reach you."

"Is that so?" Autumn humored her. "And why, exactly, is that?"

"Just bored on a Friday night, like you."

"And what makes you think I'm bored?"

"Because you're on your phone talking to a stranger," her caller purred — her voice now full of suggestion, as if this conversation were the most forbidden thing imaginable. "Nothing to do, just home from a bad blind date..."

"Who said it was bad?"

"Let's see. I talked to you, oh, two hours ago, and you're already done. *Just* enough time for dinner, probably not even dessert..."

She's good, Autumn grudgingly acknowledged.

Miss UNKNOWN went on, still in that low, self-assured voice: "I'll bet... that you even used my call as an excuse to end your date."

Silence.

"You probably said I was your sister."

Autumn was glad her mystery caller couldn't see her foolish, guilty grin.

"And that there was some kind of family emergency."

"No, I didn't, thank you very much," Autumn said triumphantly. "I said you got called in and needed me to babysit," she added with a smile.

"Ah. So now you've roped me into your web of deceit and lies. I feel *so* violated."

"Hey, *you* called *me*."

Her caller giggled. "Glad to be of service. Any time."

"Okay. Well, if you're free tomorrow night, I have another date. If things keep going the way they are..."

"You might need to be rescued?"

"Something like that."

"What time?"

"Seven."

"I'll call you at 7:45. A babysitting emergency?"

Autumn shook her head in disbelief. "Sure, why not?"

"Does that mean I get to drive the babysitter home afterward?"

"*No!*" Autumn laughed as she ended the call.

Saturday morning — one of Autumn's rather rare trips to the gym. When she got back to her car, the *Missed Call* dialog awaited her. This time, it wasn't her anonymous caller though. She clicked on the logged number to call it back.

"Hello?"

"Hey, Steph. I see you got my email."

"New number, got it. You forgot to set up your voicemail though."

"Yeah, yeah. I'll get to it someday."

"Sure you will. Promises, promises."

"Like you'd leave a message anyway."

A laugh. "Well, you got me there. What have you been up to? You've been scarce."

"Date last night."

"Ooh. Any juicy deets?"

"Yeah. About his job. And his rent-controlled loft. And what a great deal he got on his car."

"So, your life is boring as usual."

Autumn thought about the mysterious phone calls. "Well, not *completely*."

"Oh? More fun dates lined up?"

"Probably not. Hey, Steph... do you know if there's any way to get someone's phone number when they call you from a private number?"

"Hmm." She could almost "hear" her friend frowning thoughtfully. "I don't think so. I think you can block it so your phone won't accept private numbers. Why do you ask?"

Autumn gave Stephanie an edited version of the anonymous calls she'd gotten — leaving out the suggestive comments the caller had made.

"Oh. Wow. Do you think it was someone you know?"

Guiltily, Autumn remembered her initial reaction to her caller. She'd assumed it had been Steph herself, playing a prank.

"No," she said, biting her lip. "I'd just gotten the phone. Nobody even had the number yet."

"And she called back again?"

"A few times."

"Damn, Autumn. Are you worried that this person might be dangerous?"

Autumn frowned, considering the suggestion only briefly — she'd used the *UNKNOWN CALLER* as a pretext to "bail out" of her awful date, and had even

13

invited her to call again tonight in anticipation of her next crash-and-burn.

"No, I don't think so. Not at all."

Stephanie sounded doubtful. "Okay. If you say so. You busy tonight?"

"Another date."

"I thought you said you didn't have—"

"You asked if I had any more *fun* dates," Autumn clarified. "The way my luck has been..."

"I hear ya. Want me to text you about a sick aunt? Or some sort of dire emergency?"

"No, I'll be okay." Autumn decided not to mention that she'd already set up a "bail out plan" with her new "friend."

"Okay. Let's hang out soon, though, okay?"

"Sure thing!"

Autumn checked the clock. 7:51 p.m. Her blind date

was thirty-four minutes in — and, he'd now called his mother *four times*. Her phone hadn't rung — so much for her rather freaky "wrong number" dialer.

Dammit! I knew I should have had Stephanie call me.

"Are you having a good time?"

"Yes, great." Autumn smiled distractedly.

Their server came by with a carafe of wine.

"No, thanks, I'm good."

"Are you sure?" her date prompted. "My mom always said a glass of wine with dinner was great for one's health."

You don't say?

In her purse, the phone went off. *Thank God!* She fished it out — *UNKNOWN CALLER*. As she answered it, she realized she didn't even know her "friend's" name.

"Hello?"

The sultry — and now very welcome — voice oozed from the phone. "Hi there. Did I interrupt something hot and heavy?"

"Hi... sis!" she spoke loudly. "Good to talk to you!"

Her counterpart took the cue. "Hey, how's my beautiful... sexy sister?"

"I'm doing great, sis!" Autumn smiled apologetically at her date. "Everything okay?"

"Not really. I'm in a bind..."

Autumn frowned accordingly as she listened.

"Cinnamon came down with some kind of rash, and Honey Mounds is two weeks late... and now I've gotta pull a double at the Sugar Shack!"

Despite her best efforts to remain serious, Autumn felt her lips twisting into a grin.

"I'm gonna need you to babysit."

"You're gonna need me to babysit?" Autumn struggled to keep a straight face.

"Either that or come down here and do twelve lap dances! That's how many more I need to cover the rent."

Now Autumn burst into laughter.

"What's so funny, child? I gotta shake these Double-D's while I still can. Gravity's a real motherfucker!"

"Oh my God, *stop*," begged Autumn, tears running down her cheeks as her bewildered date looked on.

"Will you *help* a girl in her time of desperate need? Please hurry before the glue on these pasties wears off."

"Yes, I'll be there." She hung up, fighting to regain her composure. Once she'd done so, she gave her date a wan smile. "I gotta go. My sister needs me to babysit."

"Now?" She nodded. "But... the wine hasn't even come yet!"

"Have your mom come down," Autumn suggested, making a dash for it as she again erupted into uncontrollable laughter.

"He called his mother *four times*?"

"Four times," Autumn reiterated.

"*Nuh uh.*"

"Four times."

"Well, I guess I called just in time then."

"Yeah. Thanks..." She trailed off expectantly. *This is the part where you tell me your name.*

"Any more dates coming up?"

"No. I don't know." Autumn sighed. "I just keep picking the wrong type of guys."

"Maybe," her caller suggested thoughtfully, "that's your trouble. You're looking for the right *guy*. Maybe you should just be looking for the right *person*."

"I'm straight," asserted Autumn in a no-nonsense tone.

Her new friend laughed softly into the phone. "So is spaghetti. Until it gets wet..."

"Uh..." But the phone was flashing the *CALL ENDED* message.

Just before bedtime: *UNKNOWN CALLER.*

"May I help you?"

"Loaded question."

"It's late. Don't you have anything better to do on a Saturday night—"

"—*Than you? Nope.*"

"I was just about to go to—" Autumn stopped short. The word *bed* would certainly open up a Pandora's Box of innuendos, flirtation, and suggestive remarks from her slightly off-kilter phone-friend, who apparently wanted to "do" her on a Saturday night. "—sleep," she finished cautiously.

"Sorry your date didn't go well."

"Eh, it's ok."

"It's not you."

"Sometimes I wonder."

"*I* think you're nice. If it means anything."

A brief silence. Autumn smiled. "It does."

"Good."

"And thanks for bailing me out."

"Ah, that's right. You do owe me, don't you?"

"Uh... well, I said thanks..."

"I know. But—"

"What did you have in mind?" Autumn wasn't sure she wanted to know.

"I was thinking... you could wish me good night. And sweet dreams."

"Uh, sure. Well, um, good night."

"And...?"

"Um, sweet dreams."

"Sweet dreams for you too."

But Autumn laid awake for some time after the *CALL ENDED* notification disappeared. Thinking about life in general, her dating catastrophes, and her mysterious new "friend."

Eleven thirty a.m. The sun was already high in the sky. Exhaustion had caught up with Autumn, and she'd slept in. Checking her phone, she saw she'd missed a couple of calls, although none from her *UNKNOWN* friend. She clicked voicemail, then remembered she hadn't set it up yet.

"Coffee first," she groaned aloud.

Two cups later, she tackled it.

"Hi, this is Autumn! I can't talk right now, but you know what to do!" Satisfied, she chose *Save Greeting*.

While she was doing dishes, the phone rang. It went to her newly-configured voicemail before she could get to it though. She checked the screen. *Missed call: UNKNOWN*

With surprise, Autumn realized she was just the tiniest bit disappointed that she'd missed the call. A few seconds later, though, she was startled as the phone buzzed and chimed in her hand. *New Messages: (1)*

She clicked, thumbing the speakerphone as well. That now-familiar, soft, feminine voice filled the living room.

"No, I *don't* know what to do," the message playfully

mocked her voicemail greeting. "Maybe you need to *show* me. *Show* me, Autumn." Next, her caller launched into an obnoxious, full-blown fake orgasm. "Ohhh. Ohhhhhh…. *Ooooooooooh!*"

At least, Autumn assumed it was fake. *Nothing would surprise me at this point.*

As the recording ended, Autumn rolled her eyes... but clicked the smart key for *Save Message.*

Autumn spent Sunday handling a few errands, but mostly chilling out. The evening included a rare second date with Chaz, a guy she'd gone out with a couple weeks before. The chemistry hadn't been breathtaking, she recalled, but at least he didn't have a mommy fixation and wasn't in love with his car. Eight p.m. found her mingling at a party for one of Chaz's coworkers, rocking her black skater dress.

"You look nice tonight," Chaz complimented.

"Thanks."

Abruptly, he was kissing her. She leaned into him,

returning it. Chaz didn't seem quite sure where to put his hands. They ended up on her shoulders, although Autumn would have been okay with a little more. But the kissing was nice, especially since most of her recent dates hadn't even made it that far.

I wonder how she'd kiss me? The thought popped into her head out of nowhere, taking her somewhat by surprise and pausing her.

"You okay?"

"Uh huh. Kiss me." She pressed back against him, also taking his hands and moving them to her hips. He turned it up a notch, kissing harder and pushing her against the wall.

She'd feel soft...

Autumn involuntarily moaned at the random thought. Chaz took this as a "green light," kissing her deeper while his hands slid up and down her sides, eventually heading in the direction of her breasts. She glanced around to make sure they were still alone in the hallway but let him feel her up a little.

He moved down, graduating to kissing her neck. His

stubble was rough and scratchy against her.

She'd be nice and smooth, Autumn pondered, again shocked at herself for going there. "*Stop* it," she chided herself out loud.

"Huh?" Chaz looked up. To his credit, he *did* immediately remove his hands.

"Not you." She lifted her chin, grasping his head to gently pull him back to what he'd been doing, and nudging his hand back toward her chest.

It didn't progress much further than that. After a few more bouts of kissing (and one politely declined hand on her thigh), they made their way back to the party proper, enjoying a few more drinks and socializing a bit longer. Before too long, the party began to dissipate, as Sunday night parties often do when the attendees have the work week in front of them.

"Wanna go somewhere?" Chaz asked.

"Nah, I'm beat. I'm going to call it a night."

He nodded. "I'll give you a ride home?"

"I'm just gonna walk. It's not far." She kissed him on

the cheek. "I had a good time though."

"Me too."

She let him kiss her again, a lengthy kiss before she broke away.

"Call me." Autumn made her exit, enjoying the fresh air as she walked home.

UNKNOWN CALLER.

"Hello..."

"Hi, Autumn."

How does she know my name? A moment of alarm — until she reminded herself that it was part of her voice greeting.

"Uh, hi..."

"How was your day?"

"It was okay. Just a lazy Sunday."

"Back to work tomorrow?"

Autumn hesitated, wary about giving too much information to a stranger.

Oh, come on, most people have to go to work tomorrow. That's hardly classified information, Autumn. Besides, she'd *already* offloaded the 411 on her two catastrophic dates.

"Yep. Back to the grind."

"Me too."

"Back to the 'Sugar Shack'?" Autumn joked.

"You know it. Weekdays are the *worst*. Very few lap dances. Mostly middle-aged married men. Ugh."

Autumn found herself wondering if her "friend" *did* work at such an establishment, and actually thought about asking. Miss UNKNOWN beat her to it.

"No. I don't really work there." She laughed, a wonderful, melodious sound.

"No judgment," Autumn kidded her. "You can tell me..."

"Nah. I don't give my lap dances to just anyone."

"Okay."

A silence.

"Something on your mind, Autumn?"

Yeah. About that... "Well... I don't even know your name. You know mine."

"You left it on your voice message, silly." She seemed thoughtful. "Trying to figure out what name you should be screaming?"

"No."

"Ah, so you're a moaner, then?"

"No." Autumn gave a nervous laugh. "I told you, I'm straight."

"I know you are." Her caller's tone, though, said *keep telling yourself that.*

"Anyway, I guess I should be getting to bed. To sleep," she clarified.

"What do you think my name is?"

How the hell am I supposed to know that? "I have no idea... I mean... you just called me up, with a wrong number..."

"I know that, silly. I meant, if you had to guess my name."

Autumn thought for a second. "You sound like a 'Heather'," she guessed.

A thoughtful laugh. "That's a pretty name. But, no."

Well, all right then. I'll just keep guessing from the ten thousand other possibilities.

"I did know a 'Heather' once..."

Hmmm. How well did you know her? Autumn wondered.

"I don't—"

"Jessica. My name is Jessica."

"That's a pretty name too," Autumn complimented.

"So's Autumn."

"Thank you. Jessica," she added. "Is that 'Jess' for short?"

"Hmm."

Autumn could almost hear her friend's frown—clearly, Jessica was *not* fond of the shortened version of her name. *Got it.* "Jessica, it is!" She paused, reflecting. "So. Jessica. Do you *always* strike up conversations with your wrong numbers?"

"Just the ones I like. You know what they say..."

Autumn didn't. "What's that?"

"Sometimes wrong just feels so right." Jessica had that flirty tone again. Autumn felt herself beginning to blush.

"Autumn?"

"Yeah."

"Do you always *answer* your wrong number calls?"

"If it gets me out of a horrible date, sure!"

Jessica gave an exaggerated sniffle. "So, you're just... *using* me? I'm your bail out plan? Is that it?"

"Any port in a storm," Autumn teased.

"And I thought we had something special, Autumn."

I like it when she says my name.

"I also answer them if I think they'll be... interesting." Autumn smiled.

"Oooooh. So, I'm interesting?"

"I'd have to say so. Yes, definitely interesting, that's for sure."

"So, if you think I'm interesting, then that must mean you're interest**ed**."

"I mean... you're... fun to talk to," stammered Autumn.

"You, too."

"But I should be getting to— getting some rest. Six o'clock comes early."

"Yeah. *Hate* it when things come early."

"Uh..."

"Autumn?"

"Yes?"

"*You* can call me Jess if you want."

"Okay."

"Good night, Autumn. Sweet dreams."

"Good night, Jessica. Jess."

Autumn went to bed but found herself lying awake thinking about her mysterious caller. *Do I know her from somewhere? Did we meet before?* It was highly unlikely, though. Once more, she reminded herself that when Jessica had first called, she'd just gotten the new phone number and hadn't even given it to anyone yet.

More likely, Jess had genuinely meant to call someone else — either the previous owner of Autumn's phone number, or just an honest misdial.

This, in turn, led to speculation about whom Jessica had been trying to reach in the first place. A friend?

More than a friend?

The second thought sent a tiny pang through Autumn. Anxiety, and almost... jealousy?

You don't even know her, she chided herself. *Plus, you're straight.*

So is spaghetti, until it gets wet, her active imagination immediately replayed Jessica's suggestive remark from yesterday.

Stop it. But she found herself squirming beneath the covers as she went over the "Jessica encounters" in her head. With an effort, she willed herself to think about other things. The date with Chaz—that had been nice. Next time, Autumn pondered, she'd let him drive her home, or walk her home. And just maybe, she'd ask him if he wanted to come up for a drink.

"*Now* we're talking," she murmured. Although she was alone, she glanced around before opening her nightstand for the special "friend" she kept there. Soon, the familiar buzzing sound filled the room as she slipped out of her panties, guiding the vibrator between her thighs and teasing her slit. She was already wet, and as she traced her lips with the vibe, she tried to tell herself that the thoughts of Chaz had gotten her aroused. The kissing... his hands on her... the images of what he'd do with her.

But, try as she might, she was unable to prevent her mind from coming back to her "phone friend." That smooth, sexy voice, so self-assured, suggesting that its owner knew exactly what she wanted.

Me...

The thought made Autumn's naked body warm, and

one part of her in particular definitely took notice. She slid her toy a little farther up to address the need. "*Oooooooh, Chaz,*" she purred to the empty room. "Yes, get your tongue on it. *Mmmmmmm!*"

She pushed her head back into the pillow, hips arching slightly to meet the wonderful sensation of the toy pressing against her swollen clit. Closing her eyes, she pictured her date, looking up at her from down there, his tongue skillfully working her over.

"*Taste me...*"

She rubbed herself faster, still fantasizing about Chaz — or, trying to.

Does Jessica have long hair? Will it tickle my thighs while she goes down on me?

She forced the thought away, willing herself to return to her fantasy. "Chaz, I want you to *fuck* me," she growled forcefully. Accordingly, she moved the vibrator down, easing it between her lips and then burying it in her aching pussy. "*Ooooooooh! Yes! FUCK* me!"

That's right, she reflected triumphantly, *there's just* no *substitute for a nice hard fuck.*

33

She churned the vibrator around, her wrist moving deftly to work the buzzing, pulsing artificial cock in and out. *Ooooooh, right* there.

But despite her best efforts, those thoughts kept pervading her consciousness.

Jessica in her bed.

Jessica kissing her.

Jessica, between her thighs, looking up at her with a self-assured, sexy, confident smile, which Autumn was sure would match her voice.

"Chaz... take me..."

I could lick you while he fucks you, Jessica murmured in her head. *Nothing wrong with sharing...*

Stop it!

Autumn lifted her head and beat it against the pillow twice. She continued fucking herself with the vibrator, but now moved her free hand to her clit, picking up where the toy had left off. Now she was nailing herself in just the right spot, the slightly curved tip of the vibe aligned nicely to hit her just right.

"Almost... *there...*"

Her fingers moved faster on her button. Now that the vibrator was where she wanted it, she pressed it against her g-spot and held it there, letting loose with a scream that probably woke up half of her apartment complex. Quickly, she clamped her thighs together, holding the toy in place long enough to grab her pillow and pull it up over her face to muffle herself. Her hand went back to the round handle of the vibrator, applying more pressure. Autumn delivered a fresh volley of screams as her pussy throbbed against the vibrating silicone cock. The pillow wasn't doing much to keep her quiet, so she bit into the soft fabric, going faster.

"*MMMMMMMMMMMM!!!!*" *Almost there...* Now she was thrashing wildly, bucking against both of her talented hands.

"*Fuck me, Jess!*" she screamed into the pillow before she could catch herself. This time, instead of suppressing the thought of her "friend," though, she let it in. It was Jessica's mouth on her right now, deliciously working her over while making love to her with the vibrator. Jessica...

"*OHHHHHHHHH!*" She boiled over, coming hard, and gushing all over the vibrator and her fingers. Her juices flowed in a torrent down her thighs. She kept pressing — and kept coming. At some point, the pillow slid off. Autumn was quivering and shaking uncontrollably. Dimly, she was aware of a neighbor banging on a wall or a ceiling, and she tried to put a lid on her screaming, although without too much success.

Gradually, she came down, though she continued to be rocked with "aftershock" orgasms. Autumn slowly pulled the vibrator out, tossing it on the bed, still strumming away. After she was able to catch her breath somewhat, she fumbled for the toy, and groped at the control dial with shaky fingers. After a few tries, she was able to shut it off.

It was still several minutes before Autumn was able to move. Beneath her, the sheets were saturated—a trip to the laundry room would definitely be in order. She eased herself off the bed and stripped it, noting that her excitement had soaked through to the mattress. *I'll need to scrub that too,* she frowned.

But that would have to wait. Now that she'd gotten her release, she was starting to feel drowsy. She grabbed a couple of towels, laid them over the wet spot and curled up with her comforter.

My God, did I really say her name? But before she could reflect too deeply, sleep overtook her.

"Good morning, sunshine."

Clutching the smartphone with one hand, Autumn rubbed the sleep from her eyes with the other. "Hi."

"How'd you sleep?"

"I... slept okay."

"Any wet dreams about me?"

Autumn blushed as she eyed the makeshift bedsheet arrangement, and the towels on the mattress, necessitated by her bedtime "activities." The vibrator was still lying on the bed, and although Jess wouldn't be able to see it, Autumn felt the irrational need to deftly hide it beneath the pillow.

Phone against her ear, she came to a sitting position on the edge of the bed. The sheets and linens were crumpled on the floor where she'd left them. She'd need to do a load of laundry, plus give the mattress a good scrub. But it would have to wait till after work.

Work, she thought suddenly, blinking her eyes to focus on the alarm clock on the nightstand. *7:44.*

"*Shit!* I'm *late!*"

"Ooooooh does that mean I'm going to be an auntie?"

Yeah, right. One has to actually be having sex for that *to happen.* "Late for *work*," she explained with slight annoyance, now up and frantically scrambling through her drawers. "I forgot to set my alarm!"

"So, in other words, you're glad I called."

Autumn didn't respond. "I'm gonna be *so* late!" She needed to be at work in sixteen minutes. And, she realized, there was no way she'd be able to get away with skipping a shower, considering last night's self-pleasuring festivities.

"Jessica, I gotta get going. I am *so* late! Still haven't even gotten a shower."

"Mmmmmmm. Can I wash your back?"

"No!"

"Your *front*?"

The unbidden thought of being covered with soap and feeling gentle but purposeful hands snaking around to caress her. Autumn suppressed it.

"Jess. I *really* have to hop in the shower."

"You could just put me on speakerphone and talk to me. Not fair that I should have to be all lonely..."

She rolled her eyes, exasperated. "It's *your* fault that I overslept in the first place!"

A long, thoughtful pause. "*Really*. And how's that, exactly?"

Too late, she realized her gaffe. *Enjoy explaining this one, Autumn!*

"We didn't talk that late last night." Another pause. "Or did you think about me after we hung up?" Quiet, sexy laughter. "Or... did you do *more* than think about me?"

"Jess! I *really* have to go. Sorry."

"Autumn—"

But Autumn thumbed the red button to end the call, grabbing a clean towel and making a mad dash for the shower. "Fuck. I'm *never* gonna make it on time."

But as she hastily lathered herself up, her thoughts returned to Jess — specifically, the offhand remarks about helping her out in the shower. Again, Autumn began to feel that familiar aching need between her legs.

Fuck it, I'm already late anyway. With a naughty smirk, she removed the shower wand from its silver holder, twisting the clear plastic control knob to its *PULSE* setting and guiding it to the area where it was most needed...

Jessica didn't call that evening. Autumn stayed in, talking to Chaz briefly and filtering through responses to her various singles ads. Few of them seemed promising.

The next morning, at precisely six thirty, the phone went off — her *UNKNOWN CALLER* again.

"Just wanted to make sure you didn't oversleep again."

Autumn had been up since 5:48 — a couple of stabs at the snooze button, but then she'd been ready to go. Now, she was already sipping her second cup of coffee.

"I'm good."

"Good. Wouldn't want to have to come over there and wake you..." Jess reflected for a moment. "Well, yeah, I would."

Autumn felt her cheeks flushing slightly.

"Did you end up late yesterday?"

"Yeah. A little."

"I'm sorry if I had anything to do with that."

"Nah." She carefully avoided the thoughts of Sunday night's wild self-pleasuring session. *Or the shower yesterday. Can't forget about that, can we?* "I showed up late, but the boss wasn't actually in till ten thirty," she explained neutrally. "So, I was okay."

"That's good."

She took a sip of her coffee. "Do you work, Jessica?"

"Yeah. Although I'm off today."

"Nice. You're up early, then?"

"Because I like talking to you."

"Oh. Well, that's... sweet."

"You're sweet, Autumn."

"Thank you." She bit her lip. "Um... you too."

"Eh." There was a pause for a few seconds, followed by a moist slurping noise. "Mmmmm. Yeah," Jess conceded, "pretty sweet today."

Autumn blushed some more, her heart beating a little faster. *Did she just...?*

"Anyway. I'd better let you get ready for work. Wouldn't want you being late again. Talk to you soon, Autumn."

"Uh, bye, Jess."

CALL ENDED. To Autumn's surprise, she felt the slightest twinge of disappointment that her friend hadn't stayed on the phone just a little longer.

That, and a twinge of something else as she replayed Jessica's conversation in her mind. Specifically, the part where the girl had almost certainly tasted herself on her own fingers.

Before she fully realized what she was going to do, Autumn slid her own hand into her shorts. She was already rather aroused and was able to easily slip two fingers in her pussy. She gave herself a few strokes, then emerged, sucking her fingers into her mouth and slurping on them.

"Pretty sweet here too, Jess," she said to the dormant phone. Purposefully she rose, the half-finished cup of coffee forgotten as she hurried to the shower to take care of business.

Slow work day. As the afternoon dragged on, Autumn found herself thinking about Jessica. In the grand scheme of things, she realized, she knew very little about her new "friend."

I don't even know where she lives. For all she knew, Jess could be on the other side of the country — or, she could be in the cubicle next to her. Without having so much as a phone number, she couldn't even do a reverse lookup or reference an area code.

So, ask for her number. The thought both excited and perturbed her. What if Jess *did* turn out to be a thousand miles away?

Why does it matter? Planning to meet her, Autumn? Let her wash your back? Find out how good she tastes?

Make spaghetti with her?

Her cheeks once more began to burn at the naughty thoughts that kept cropping up, and she found herself fidgeting in her chair.

In her bag, her cell phone rang. She checked it, somewhat disappointed that it wasn't Jessica. Rather, it was Mike, a guy she'd been trading emails with on one of the singles websites. A little bit of banter, and they set up a date for Thursday night. "See you then," she told him as she ended the call.

Jessica didn't call that night, nor the following morning. But in the late afternoon, while Autumn was coping with rush hour traffic on the way home, the smartphone went off: *UNKNOWN CALLER.*

"Hey."

"How are you doing?"

"Good. Haven't heard from you for a bit. I was wondering if you'd dumped me," she said half-jokingly.

"Oh, you don't have to worry there."

"That so?"

"Yeah." Another one of Jessica's reflective pauses — the kind that usually left Autumn wondering just *what* her phone pal might be doing over there.

"Everything... okay?"

"Huh? Oh, yeah. Had a couple people out sick and had to take a few extra shifts."

"Oh. Sorry."

"Time and a half."

"Well, that's good."

"Any more great dates?"

"Tomorrow night."

"Ooooooh. Need me on standby with a babysitting emergency?"

Autumn giggled. "Nah. I've been talking to Mike for a while. I think we'll be okay."

Abruptly, a silver Scion veered directly into her lane, cutting her off and forcing her to slam on the brakes. "Hey! *Fucker!*"

"Huh?"

"Not you, Jess," she apologized. "This idiot in front of me."

"Oh, you're driving? I'd better let you go."

"Talk tomorrow?"

"I gotta be in *real* early. I'll call tomorrow night. Maybe after your date. Bye."

"Or you could just give me your number..." But her friend had already hung up.

Thursday evening. Autumn opened her door, thankful

to be home from her latest embarrassing failure. She headed straight for the fridge, where she had a fifth of mango-flavored vodka in the freezer. Twisting the cap off, she swigged directly from the bottle. The alcohol wouldn't freeze, but the vodka had an almost gel-like viscosity. It numbed her tongue slightly as it went down.

She took a second swig before heading to her bedroom and shedding the skater dress, digging out an extra-sized T-shirt and a nondescript pair of sweat pants.

UNKNOWN CALLER, her phone abruptly signaled.

"Yeah, where were you when I needed you?" she snickered in the direction of the phone, before reminding herself she'd passed on Jessica's offer to set up a "bail out" call.

"Hello."

"How was your date?"

"I *don't* want to talk about it," Autumn declared.

"Wow. That good?"

"How was your day?"

"Long," Jess sighed. "Glad to be kicking back with a drink."

"Yeah? What do you drink?"

"I've got vodka tonight."

Grinning, Autumn toyed with the still chilly neck of the bottle next to her. "Me too. What kind?"

"I like the flavored ones. This one's pineapple."

"Me too. Although mine's mango tonight. Great minds—"

"—think alike."

"Indeed, we do," Autumn agreed wistfully.

"You okay, Autumn?"

"Yeah." She took another drink, then a deep breath. There'd be no harm in opening up. "So, this date..."

"Yeah? What happened? You said he seemed okay."

"Oh, yeah. We'd been emailing. Really nice. Polite. Not weird. Then tonight we met up."

"Weird?"

"I'll say." She giggled, still somewhat in disbelief as she reflected. "Like, a *minute* after meeting me, he decides to tell me that I'm the spitting image of this porn star he watches. Like, in what universe does a girl wanna hear this on a first date?" *Or on any date, for that matter?*

"Get the fuck out of here."

"I'm serious. And then he goes on and mentions it at least half a dozen times, all throughout dinner. 'I just can't get over it. You're a dead ringer!' he keeps saying. Oh. Except that my boobs need to be just a *little* bigger."

Jess giggled for several seconds, then cleared her throat, obviously trying to straighten up and be more supportive. "I'm sorry. I shouldn't laugh."

"It's not your fault. And then our waitress comes to our table, he watches her leave, and then starts talking about how *she* should be in porn. Because the pay would be better, and she'd get to fuck all the time."

An amused snicker. "What was her name?"

"I don't remember. She said it when she came to our table, but she wasn't wearing a nametag, so—"

"No, silly." Jess laughed. "What was the name of this porn star protégé of yours?"

"Oh." She thought for a second. "Brianna somebody. Um... Bristol. Brianna Bristol."

There was a brief silence from the other end of the line, followed by the sound of fingers typing on a keyboard. It took a few seconds for Autumn to realize what her friend was doing.

"Ooooooooh. Wow. She's hot." In the background, Autumn could hear the sound of a man talking and a woman moaning. As she suspected, Jessica had searched the name online and was now looking at porn.

"Damn." Jess whistled appreciatively. "Is that *really* what you look like?"

"I don't *know*," Autumn whined, indignant. "Jeez, it's not like I *watch* that stuff!" *Much.*

"Well, aren't you curious to see if she *does* look like you?"

"It wasn't exactly my first thought."

"She's sexy. Wait, let's see if she has more scenes."

More typing and clicking, and a minute later, Jess had something else queued up. "Ah. Oh, this one looks hot as fuck."

This one sounded different somehow, and it took Autumn a moment to pinpoint why. All of the voices, moans, and screams were feminine. Jessica had selected a girl-on-girl video.

"Um... Jess?"

"What? Oh, yeah. Sorry." A throaty, sexy chuckle. "Whew. It's getting a *little* warm over here!"

"Good to know," Autumn replied evenly, rolling her eyes. *Glad my awful dating life can entertain you.*

"Just saying. Girl, if you look *anything* like that... "

"I wouldn't know." On the unseen video, one of the girls was screaming her head off in pleasure. Autumn wondered if the set of lungs in question belonged to her doppelgänger.

"Well, aren't you at least *curious?*"

About what? Somehow, Autumn had the feeling that her friend wasn't just referring to some porn actress.

51

"Come on. Take a look."

Autumn sighed in defeat, flipping her laptop open. The familiar chime sounded off as her desktop came up.

"*That's* the spirit! Now, type in—"

"Hold on," Autumn interrupted. "This thing takes forever to load up."

"Oh, no problem. I'll just... entertain myself while we wait."

"Jess!"

The low, sexy chuckle again. "Just kidding. I'll behave myself. For now," she promised. In the background, the porn starlet was announcing that she was coming as the screams and moans continued.

Finally, the hourglass cursor went away, and Autumn double-clicked the Firefox icon. Another hourglass as the browser began to pop up.

"Any luck?"

"Firefox is loading up. This thing is *really* slow," she explained apologetically.

"No problem. I won't start without you."

Start what? "Jess, I'm just taking a look because I'm curious," she cautioned, not wanting to lead her friend on.

"Mmmmmm. I *knew* you were curious."

She blushed again. "About the actress, I mean!"

"Of course, sweetie." *Whatever you say,* the accompanying tone conceded.

The browser popped up. "Okay. Finally."

"Okay, great. Now go to www, dot pornwire, dot—"

Autumn cut her off. "How 'bout I just Google it?"

"Google? Well, that's no fun."

"Yeah, I'm kinda boring."

"Far from it, Autumn."

She clicked on the search bar and began typing. "Okay. Brianna Bristol. How do you spell it?"

"You should know. It's *your* stage name!"

"*Not,*" Autumn protested vehemently.

"Okay, okay." Jess spelled out the name, and Autumn typed it in. A number of images were returned in the search results — some from photoshoot-type websites, some a bit less "tame." She clicked one of the more conservative pictures and was rewarded with a page-full of thumbnail photos of a buxom blonde woman next to a swimming pool, wearing (and eventually removing) a pink bikini. In the face, she could see the passing resemblance — but in the chest, Autumn would have some catching up to do. Like, at least two cup sizes.

"Did you find it?"

"Yeah. She's... pretty."

"Was he right? Is that what you look like?"

Autumn snorted. "Yeah. Maybe if I were less addicted to Olive Garden — and more addicted to my gym pass. And if I had four thousand dollars for a boob job." She shrugged. "I guess in the face... yeah, kinda."

"I like."

"Good. You and my date would get along perfectly then. I'll fix you two up!"

"I don't want him, though."

Dammit, Jess. You make it really *hard to have a crappy night.* "And what *do* you want?" she asked shyly, expecting the answer to be "you."

"I want what she's getting," Jess murmured, in obvious reference to the video she was still watching. Even in the background, Autumn could tell that the starlet was "getting" plenty of whatever it was.

She asked anyway — albeit hesitantly. "And what is she getting?"

"Mmmmmm. Look up 'Brianna Bristol and Sara Belle office encounter.'"

"Um..." She was thankful her friend couldn't see how badly she was blushing. "I'll... go ahead and take your word for it."

"Suit yourself. It could be fun."

"I'll just have to take your word for it."

"Okay then. In that case, I think I'm going to have to take a shower."

"Have fun."

"You sure you don't want to... help one another out?"

Autumn wasn't sure at all. But, "I'll... have to pass, for now."

"Hmmmmm. For *now*, huh? Guess I'll just have to step up my game."

"Jess..."

"Bye, Autumn. Or should I call you, Brianna?"

"Nooooo," Autumn giggled. "Go... do whatever. Have fun."

"Bye, sweetie."

After the call ended, Autumn found herself wishing her sexy phone friend had pushed just a *little* harder.

Or that you hadn't chickened out, Autumn. She held the phone in her hand, hoping it would go off again with those words UNKNOWN CALLER. But it didn't.

Probably because she's having fun. Without me, to boot.

After a long while, she set the phone down, took

another generous shot of the vodka, and went back to her keyboard. Clicking in the search tool, she modified her previous query to add:

sara belle office encounter

The first return led her to a porn site. A video window featured a freeze frame of the blonde she'd already searched facing a curvy brunette in an office setting. Beneath it, a caption described: "Party animal Brianna Bristol is late for work again! Coworker Sara Belle is tired of picking up the slack for lazy Brianna. When her friend sneaks into the office, Sara is ready and waiting for her."

Typical. Autumn chuckled at the cliché. When she clicked on the *play* triangle at the center of the video image, she was almost able to convince herself it was *just* for a laugh at the expense of the stereotypically bad plot.

The movie clip opened with an ad spot of a sultry, bikini-clad blonde, with impossibly red lips, urging the viewer to visit a website to "meet sluts near you." This faded out, and the movie opened. The counter at the bottom advised the clip was twenty-two minutes long.

Jess could still be watching it. The thought sent a silent jolt through her, finishing up between her legs.

The video predictably began with "Brianna" sneaking into an office, without any real effort at being clandestine. As expected, "Sara" caught her in the act, complete with a loud *"Hold it!"* at a decibel level that would never occur in a real office setting. For that matter, Autumn mused, if she were to show up at *her* office dressed like either of these two girls, she'd certainly find herself sent home, probably with a final paycheck in hand.

Suspend your disbelief, Autumn, the voice of her crotchety, hundred-year-old high-school English teacher chided in her head.

On the screen, the brunette was sternly lecturing her "subordinate" about responsibility. Although she was in "serious trouble," the Brianna actress was unable to refrain from smirking and grinning foolishly throughout the admonishing. Before too long, it became apparent to Sara that her lecturing was going nowhere, and she then informed Brianna she was due "something for her trouble."

"What do you mean?" Brianna and Autumn murmured simultaneously, the latter bursting into laughter at how predictable this stuff was.

As it turned out, although the dress code at Sara's office called for black thigh-highs and four-inch pumps, it did *not* call for panties — this became immediately apparent when she draped her legs over the arms of the leather office chair and "forced" Brianna to her knees.

"*Do it* if you want to keep your job!" Sara warned.

"Please, I *need* this job," Brianna whined desperately, smiling.

"Then get that tongue busy!" The brunette's acting was slightly less horrible — she actually managed to avoid laughing as she said her lines. She grabbed a handful of blonde hair and pulled her subordinate between her thighs. Brianna eagerly dived in, moaning emphatically as "Sara" instructed her charge to "*Lick it good, you slut!*"

Jessica had me in mind when she was watching this. That means she was imagining me doing... that... to her. Autumn didn't even realize that her hand had slipped beneath the waistband of her sweat pants.

There was, indeed, lots of screaming. At first, it was streaming through her laptop's built-in speakers, but before long, Autumn was adding "music" of her own.

"*Ohhhhh,* Jessica,... you taste so fucking good," she groaned as her fingers deftly found their mark. "So fucking *hot...*"

The scene shifted, as the dominant Sara pulled Brianna up from her kneeling position, sitting her atop the desk and spreading her thighs.

"Oh, *yeah,* Jess, please taste me, need it *so bad...*" She slid a second hand into her pants, expertly pleasuring both her clit and her lips. Autumn followed the on-screen action, meshing it into her own forbidden fantasy. Soon, Brianna was laid lengthwise across the desk, her coworker climbing up to straddle her face in some sixty-nine action.

"Oh *Jessica... Jess...*"

Now she was picturing her friend doing that to her — and her reciprocating. Autumn had no experience, true — but she'd be able to take her cues from Jessica, right?

What she does to me, I'll do to her.

Oh fuck, I can almost feel *her mouth on me.*

Jessica...

"*Jessica!!!*" She was screaming it now. The porn starlets on her screen were still going at it, but she was no longer paying attention — her *own* imagination had taken over.

"*Show me what you like, Jess...*" She moaned it aloud as her fingers continued their pleasuring. "*Ohhhhhhh!*"

Her timing was impeccable. Just as the two actresses in her video burst into simultaneous fake orgasms, Autumn delivered one of her own; except, of course, hers was the genuine article.

"Jessica," she sighed as she collapsed in her chair, satisfied and content.

12:31 a.m.: *UNKNOWN CALLER.* Although Autumn was in bed, she wasn't asleep. She reached for the phone, then stopped. Then reached for it again, hovered her finger above the green button... and, ultimately, pressed the red to send Jess to voicemail.

She'd gone to bed an hour and a half ago, but her mind had been racing, and now continued to do so.

What am I doing?

I'm straight.

It's just flirting; it doesn't mean anything.

She probably lives two thousand miles away.

Chaz is really nice. What's wrong with him?

I said her name.

I don't know her. What if she's some crazy person?

I screamed *her name.*

Listen to me. I'm *some crazy person.*

I have a date tomorrow. With a guy.

I should have picked up her call. What if she stops calling? I don't even know how to get in touch with her.

I wonder if she'd go slow with me at first...

Fuck, I'm so confused.

The phone vibrated again. *UNKNOWN CALLER.*

I can't talk to her. Not right now.

Her thumb hesitated over the red icon.

If I give her the "fuck off" button again, what if she gets mad and doesn't call back?

Autumn waited for a few more rings, so that Jess would assume she was just asleep, and then thumbed the hang-up.

Chicken.

Her mind continued to run rampant, although Jessica didn't call back. Finally, Autumn drifted off to sleep amid warm thoughts of her mysterious "friend."

PART TWO

GAMES

Five thirty a.m. *Way too early. Hello, snooze button! See you in nine minutes.*

At 5:39 a.m., Autumn sat up and stretched. On her phone, she saw she had a voicemail.

Wow, someone's an early bird.

She played the message and was rewarded with Jessica's vibrant voice.

"You wake up to some *activity* beneath your covers. At first, you assume it's that guy you came home with last night. Then you remember he left after that make out session on the couch." A pause. "As you feel yourself being kissed and licked down there... you hear moaning from beneath the sheets. *Feminine* moaning."

Autumn squirmed as she continued listening to the message.

"You say my name. Questioningly. I don't answer, I just giggle. That, and well, my mouth is quite busy at the moment."

"Jess!" Autumn hissed into the phone, although she was talking to a voicemail.

"You want to reach down and stop me. But Autumn... I'm *really* good at what I'm doing... mmmmm... And you're *so* delicious, by the way..."

Fuck. Autumn's hand, having a mind of its own, was already slipping into the waistband of the cutoff sweat shorts she'd worn to bed.

"You also see some rustling beneath the blankets farther down. That's right, I'm taking care of me, too, Autumn..."

I should hang up.

Yeah, right, *Autumn.*

"My moaning is getting louder. And so is yours... Oh, baby, it's like music..." Another brief pause, filled with heavy breathing and moaning. "My hand, the one that's *not* occupied" — Jess giggled at this — "slips out from beneath the sheets. Pulling your nightstand drawer open, looking for the special *friend* I know you keep in there. Mmm, baby. Let's see if we can make Autumn late for work again. "

The voicemail was punctuated by Jessica moaning and eventually screaming Autumn's name. After that, there was a "Hope you have a wonderful day, Autumn! Don't play too hard!" and then the message ended.

"Dammit, Jess," Autumn cursed as she made a beeline for her shower, fumbling her shorts and her already damp panties off along the way. Her friend had gotten one thing right. She was, indeed, going to be running late this morning.

Eight fifteen p.m. Autumn, at the TGI Friday's bar, on her third drink —alone.

No-call, no-show. Way to help a gal's self-esteem.

She stirred the ice with her straw, reflecting on yet another demoralizing failure. Tony had sounded promising — and, while she hadn't been the best judge of character of late, he could have at least *shown up*.

Joke's on you, Tony. Because you *would probably have gotten* lucky*!* It was partially the alcohol talking, Autumn knew, but hadn't she come here with something to prove? She reflected back on her day. In the morning, she'd ducked another Jessica call, feeling very awkward about the illicit thoughts and fantasies she'd had (and played out during her solo session). *It's just some good old-fashioned sexual frustration,* she'd told herself in the car on the way to work. Again while sitting at her desk as the day crawled by. And again during the rush-hour commute home. *Your dating track record has been horrid recently. Jessica is new and exciting, so naturally your mind is going to wander there.*

So, as she'd stood in front of her vanity, dolling herself up, Autumn had resolved that tonight would be the night to get herself back "on track," albeit at the expense of her blind date.

Great plan, Autumn.

The bartender came over. "Another one?"

She scowled. "No, I think I get the message." Downing the rest of her Long Island, she fished out a twenty and tossed it on the bar. "Thanks."

Twenty minutes later, her Uber dropped her off at home. *Terrific, another boring Friday night.* Once more, she went inside and headed straight for the vodka. Having killed the mango one, she'd followed Jessica's lead and went for pineapple this afternoon when she'd done her spot-shopping.

Two swigs in, and the phone buzzed.

"Hello."

"Hi, stranger."

"Hi, Jess."

"No date tonight?"

"Apparently not," Autumn sighed, proceeding to tell Jessica about tonight's date. Or the lack thereof.

"He stood you up? Hmph." Silence for a moment. "I'm sorry, sweetheart."

"Not your fault." Autumn frowned. "Sorry I haven't been around."

"Avoiding me?"

"No. Not trying to, anyway. Just..." *Feeling awkward about the thoughts I'm having about you.*

"I understand."

Autumn had another helping of the vodka. Apparently, her friend caught this. "What are we drinking?"

"More vodka."

"Love it. What flavor?"

"Pineapple this time." *Great. Now she's going to think I'm weird, or that I'm fixated on her and want to copy her.* But then, she reminded herself that it was Jess who kept calling. *Not that I mind at this point.*

"Pineapple, hmmm?"

"Yup."

"I'm starting to rub you off. I mean, uh," Jess amended hastily, "starting to rub off on you." Although her friend stammered this, Autumn had the distinct impression that the Freudian slip had been on purpose.

"Uh, yeah." She took another drink. "Good stuff."

"I just poured myself a shot too."

"Well, you have lots of catching up to do." She told Jessica about the Long Island Iced Teas she'd downed during her frustrating non-date.

"I'd better get started then." The low, sexy chuckle

again. "Do you promise not to take advantage of me?"

Autumn gave a wistful laugh. "I don't know. At this point..." She trailed off.

"Okay. Well, if we're drinking, we should toast. Raise your glass!"

"I'm, well, drinking straight from the bottle tonight," Autumn confessed.

"Lush," Jess teased. "Well, then, raise your *bottle*."

"K. Got it."

"To friends."

And, Autumn realized, even behind the flirting, the pseudo-anonymity of the private calls, and the overall mystery, Jessica *was* a friend. Someone who took time out to call, check up on her, laugh with — and sometimes at — her. On the heels of that, she felt awful about having avoided Jessica's calls.

Don't get all misty-eyed, you big baby. Nevertheless, she had to swallow a lump in her throat. "To *true* friends."

"Hear, hear." They drank.

"No plans for you on a Friday night?"

"Yes, I do, actually..."

Autumn couldn't help but feel a touch of disappointment. Until Jess went on. "I'm spending it with you."

"That's so sweet. But you don't have to."

"But I want to." She could hear Jessica's smile through the phone. "Let's play a game, Autumn."

"What, uh, kind of game?"

"A game called Truth or Dare."

Autumn giggled. "Yeah, maybe if we were in high school."

"It'll be fun."

"Oh, I'm sure it will." She took another drink, thinking about it. Jess would almost certainly test her boundaries with some naughty questions. But, on the obverse, *Autumn* would be able to ask away as well, and perhaps learn more about her mysterious "friend."

And it's not like I have anything better to do. "Okay, what the hell."

"That's the spirit. I'll even let you go first."

"How nice of you. Okay, it's been a *long* time. I don't even remember how to do this."

"I'm sure you do. They say you never forget, it's like riding a bicyc— oh, wait, that's sex."

Laughing, Autumn cleared her throat. "Okay. So, I just—"

"Ask me a question."

"Okay." She brainstormed for a question that would be in the "spirit" of the game, but not too raunchy. "Do you... have any tattoos?"

"I have two. A rose on my lower leg. And... a heart."

Autumn swallowed. "Where?" she asked casually.

"It would be easier to show you than tell you."

"Easier? How so?"

"Well, okay, I meant *more fun.*" A laugh. "My turn." Jessica's voice dropped to a low, secretive murmur. "Have you ever had a one-night stand?"

Although she felt slightly abashed, Autumn plodded ahead. "Um... well, how would you... you know, define... I mean, I do online dating, you know."

"Actual sex," Jess clarified. "Going to second base or giving a BJ to some stranger on craigslist doesn't count. Not that I'm suggesting you'd ever do something of the sort."

"Oh, no, not innocent little me." Autumn grinned.

"We're talking intercourse on the first date followed by never seeing them again."

"Well." Autumn smiled. "I *do* have the 'never seeing them again' part down pretty well. But, no, I do *not* sleep with guys on the first date."

"You don't sleep with *guys* on the first date. Noted." Jessica chuckled thoughtfully. Before her friend could run off on some sapphic tangent with this, Autumn put on her thinking cap again.

"Okay. Jessica. Have you ever had a crush on a celebrity?"

"Brianna Bristol," Jess sang out immediately. "She's this porn star whom I recently discovered…"

Blushing, Autumn recollected the "adventure" prompted by the X-rated movie the night before.

"Are you a moaner or a screamer, Autumn?"

"Screamer, definitely." She grinned.

"Mmmmmm."

"In fact," she confided slyly, loosening up with some help from the vodka, "recently, I had a time where I got so loud, I had to put a pillow over my face."

"*How* recently was that?"

"Uh…" Autumn stammered. "I don't think you're allowed to ask more questions after I answer."

"Fair enough. For now. Is it your turn?"

Relief. "Yeah. Let me think."

"Give it to me, Autumn." The young woman tried to pretend that her friend was referring to *just* a party-game question.

"Sex in public, ever?"

"Public, as in...?"

"Let's say, somewhere with more risk of being caught?"

"Nice." Jessica pondered this. "Okay, not sure if you'd quite call this 'public' but... I brought this guy home for the holidays."

"You mean, like in a boyfriend capacity?"

"Hush, you're not allowed to ask more questions." Autumn's own words were used to rebuke her. "It was a sort of arrangement. I wasn't seeing him per se, but I have one of those families where they obsess over whether I'm going to be single forever. When I'm going to settle down and stuff."

"Oh, you mean your family doesn't know that you're—"

"I'm *not* gay," Jess interrupted reproachfully. "I like both. But it's more of a matter of wanting to find the right person" — there was that phrase again — "before tying myself down. And not allowing my mother to pressure me into feeling like I *have* to have a man in my life. But, anyway, I showed up at the holidays, with the guy in tow, everyone's happy that Jessica is on the right track."

"And...?"

"Well, he deserved *something* for his trouble." A low, satisfied moan as Jess reflected. "In my old bedroom, I have this four-poster canopy bed. He told me his fantasy was to tie a woman to a bed like that. Well..."

"He got his wish?"

Jess giggled. "And then some. We fucked while my whole family was downstairs working on Thanksgiving dinner. The 'risk of getting caught' part was that my door at home does *not* lock. Or even close all the way." She laughed seemingly as she thought about it. "Does that answer your question?"

"I'd say so." Autumn grinned, fanning herself.

"Good. I aim to please," Jessica purred suggestively. "My turn again. Have you ever been with a woman, Autumn?"

"I told you, I'm—"

Jess laughed. "I know. Have you ever done anything with a girl?"

"No." Autumn wished she could give Jess an answer that would thrill her, rather than coming across as Ms. Boring. "I haven't even kissed another girl yet." *Sorry to be a Debbie Downer.*

But Jessica, ever the life of the party, focused only on the last word. "Mmmmm. I like that 'yet' part."

Did I say that? "I meant—"

"Mmm-hmm. Freudian slip, Autumn?" Again, the sexy, assured laugh that went right to Autumn's core, melting her.

"My turn," she stammered. *Pretty sure what* her *answer to the same question would be, so...* "Tell me about the first time you... uh, kissed a girl." Now, Autumn was *really* feeling like this was high school.

"Growing up, I wasn't too popular. I was kind of awkward. Well, one day I managed to invite myself to this party. The kind where they played little games like Seven Minutes in Heaven. You know that one?"

Autumn grinned. She indeed remembered it.

"The 'cool kids' thought it would be hilarious to send me into the closet with another girl. Someone else who wasn't really allowed at the 'cool table.' Heather Barnes."

"Heather..."

"Yes. That's why I thought it was funny the time I asked you to guess my name and you said Heather."

"So, you were in the closet with..."

"Yeah. Only it backfired on the cool kids. Because I totally didn't mind."

"You knew right away?"

"After a few seconds. Kissing a girl is totally different than a guy. Not that I'd had loads of experience by then."

"What about, um, Heather?"

"After about a minute, she ran her fingers through my hair and said, 'Oh my God,' and ran from the closet screaming. To this day, though, I think she knew right away, but wanted to keep going."

"Oh, my. And what about, like, when was the first

time you... you know, did more?"

Jessica *tsk*ed at her. "Well, you'll have to ask that when it's your turn again, won't you?"

"No, it's not a big deal," Autumn clarified quickly. "I just... was making conversation…"

"I see. Well, speaking of conversing... Hmm, let's see. Truth or Dare. Have you ever said my name while pleasuring yourself?"

Autumn's face turned red as she recounted a couple of the "adventures" she'd had. The night she'd watched the porn scene at Jessica's suggestion, and the time she'd reduced her sheets and her mattress to swampland. Not to mention the shower.

"I'm waiting."

"I'm thinking!" Autumn responded defensively.

Sweet laughter. "What's there to think about, Autumn? It's a pretty straightforward question."

"I'm gonna... can I take my chances with the Dare?"

"Honey, you can do whatever you want."

"Like, what kind of dare would it be?"

Another chuckle. "I can't tell you that. It would defeat the purpose of playing the game, now, wouldn't it?" Sensing Autumn's uneasiness, she murmured some assurance. "Don't worry. I'll be gentle with you."

"Please do."

"So, you want the Dare then?"

"I— I guess so. Yes."

"You have to say 'Dare.'"

"D-dare."

This time, Jessica's giggling lasted for several seconds.

"What?"

"It's just that... well, the very act of ducking the question kind of answers it for me."

Autumn's cheeks grew redder. "Jess..."

"It's okay. I'm definitely not offended! We're friends here, Autumn." She stopped, seemingly to think. "Autumn's Dare. Hmm. Tell me, what are you wearing?"

Autumn described the dress, although somewhat confused — she'd expected the Dare to be an act, not another question.

"That's not your Dare, sweetheart. I just need to get an idea of what I'm working with. Wearing a bra with that?"

"No bra," she rasped, her throat slightly dry. To remedy this, she chugged a little more vodka. *I have a feeling I'm going to need it.*

"Go to the kitchen. Get a cup and put some ice in it."

"Ice?"

"Yes, dear. It happens to water when it goes below thirty-two degrees."

Shrugging, Autumn headed to the kitchen, hoping that vodka was going to be a factor in this. She grabbed a cup and held it under the dispenser on her refrigerator. "Crushed or cubed?"

"Cubed."

She pushed the dispense lever, and the chunks of ice began to rattle into the cup.

"How much ice?"

"Half full is fine."

She obeyed. Jess told her to go back to the living room.

"That's it?"

"Oh, no," sang Jess. "Most definitely *not* it. Pop your breasts out of your dress."

"*Jess!*" Autumn gasped in shock.

"Do it, baby."

Normally she would have balked. But now, she'd become comfortable enough with her phone friend to be a little bit adventurous. Plus, Autumn was buzzing nicely by now, which didn't hurt matters.

And she had to play by the rules, didn't she?

"Okay..." There were a couple of buttons in the back of the dress. Once she fumbled them undone, the front was loosened enough to pop herself free, which she did. "Okay. The gals are free."

"Mmm. How big are they?"

"Not as big as my 'protégé' as you called her. Sorry to disappoint."

"Not disappointed at all."

"Is it my turn now?" Autumn asked hopefully.

"Oh, we're not done with you yet."

Autumn didn't think she was, but it had been worth a shot.

"Grab a piece of ice, and tease your nipples with it."

"Jess!"

"C'mon, do it."

Autumn took a deep breath, then slid her hand into the cup and selected a piece of ice. Slowly, she brought it out and rubbed it against her left nipple.

"*Ooooooh,* fuck, it's *cold.*"

"It's ice, sweetie."

Autumn giggled at the sensation.

"Do both nipples. Both hands. For one turn."

"But I have to hold the phone."

Jessica gasped. "You mean you don't have any kind of headset? A Bluetooth?"

"No," she said apologetically. "I'm technologically sheltered. And, well, sheltered in other ways too."

"I'd say we're working on that. Okay. Well, alternate between them. Are your nipples getting hard?"

"Yes," Autumn confessed.

"Okay, then go ahead with my next question. But don't stop your Dare."

Autumn struggled to think. Now she was wishing that she had a handsfree headset as well so she could free up her other hand. Although, not for her other nipple. She was definitely beginning to crave *other* attention.

"Have you ever made a sex video?"

"Never with a guy." Autumn opened her mouth, but Jess cut her off. "And not with a gal either." She laughed. "I filmed myself deep throating a dildo."

"How far were you... um... able to..."

"I went all the way, honey," said Jess matter-of-factly. "My turn again. Truth or Dare. Have you ever purposely sent one of my calls to voicemail?"

Yes, but only because I was embarrassed about jilling off to you. Autumn didn't savor the thought of going into that, nor of hurting Jessica's feelings by *not* explaining herself. She stalled. "Sent to voicemail? On my phone? I think you left me a message once, is that what you mean?"

"No," Jess explained patiently, cutting through the charade. "I meant did you ever *not* want to take my call, so you hit the hang-up button to send the call to voicemail."

"Um..."

"You can always take Door Number Two. The Dare," Jessica elaborated.

"Yeah, I think... sure, why not? I'll do that."

"Are your boobs still hanging out?"

"Yes."

"Still playing with the ice?"

"Uh... yeah. Can I stop?"

"The turn is over. Yes, you may stop. But keep them hanging out."

Autumn felt a sense of relief. Boob-play wasn't that bad, and as long as Jessica continued to "be gentle" with her sheltered friend.

"Okay. Is there a window there?"

The apartment's living room featured a sliding glass door leading onto a second-story balcony, facing another apartment building in the complex and overlooking a courtyard with a walkway cutting between the two buildings. Briefly, Autumn described it.

"Perfect."

"For...?"

"Your Dare." Her tone was authoritative, no-nonsense. "Naked breasts. Against the glass for twenty seconds. Now."

Autumn's jaw dropped. "Jess, I... there are other apartments right there! And people walk by all the time on the sidewalk, I can't just—"

"Not my problem. Now, Autumn."

"I—"

"Don't make me ask again." The warning caused Autumn to quiver.

"Okay," she stammered. "Yes, Jessica, I did send you to voicemail. But just because I was feeling a little awkward about..." *About fucking myself to the thought of you.* "About some of the things we talk about."

Jess laughed. "Thank you, Autumn. I appreciate your candor. But you've *already* chosen the Dare. You can't just change back because you don't want to do it."

"But... I answered your—"

"You chose Dare*,*" Jess reminded. "Now, boobs on glass. And I do mean, mashed against the window."

"Jessica... please..."

"Go to the window, Autumn." That voice, so self-assured. And, domineering. There was no thought whatsoever of disobeying. In fact, Autumn's feet were already shuffling her in that direction. Further, in her imagination, she could envision how it would be to have Jessica give her *other* instructions — but, in person.

Nobody was in the courtyard. Across the way, though, there were lights on in many of the first- and second-floor apartments. All at once, her mind began racing off on that tangent of *she probably lives over there, a hundred feet away. I've probably seen her every day.* Despite how empirically unlikely that was.

"What's outside?"

"Nobody. But lights are on over there, people in those apartments could see..." Inspiration struck. "Jess. May I have another Dare?"

A chuckle. "You may not," her friend said, now with an inkling of wickedness.

Sighing, Autumn walked back toward the couch she'd been vegging on.

"Are you doing it?"

"Just a minute!" she retorted crossly, grabbing her vodka and taking a much-needed swig. "Okay, fine. Let's do this."

"*You're* doing it. I'm just going to listen and enjoy. And count."

She looked outside again. The "coast" was still clear. As far as she could tell.

"Okay. Twenty seconds?"

"Yes. Starting... *now.*"

Autumn sidled up to the window. She giggled nervously. "I can't believe I'm doing this."

Sighing, she pressed her boobs against the glass. Her nipples, just now getting re-acquainted with room temperature, reacted again to the cold. "Oh, you *bitch*! It's *cold*!" She giggled as her friend began counting aloud.

Nervously, she kept her eyes on the courtyard. As far as the apartments across the way, Autumn couldn't quite bring herself to look up in that direction, fearful she'd see multiple eyes staring back at the slut in Apartment 208.

Jess kept counting as Autumn fretted about how cold it was, that someone was going to see her, and that her friend was a bitch.

"You love it," Jess pointed out. "Twelve. Thirteen..."

Activity from the edge of the courtyard. "Shit, someone's on the sidewalk down there!" Somebody was, indeed, walking in her direction.

"Smile and wave to them," her naughty friend suggested. "Life is short. Fourteen..."

"Come on, they're coming. Can I stop?"

"Nope, not yet! Fifteen..."

"You twisted bitch!" But she stayed the course.

"*Nam*e-calling. Tsk, tsk. Are we quite sure that's the way to get what we want?" A pause, and then a long, deliberately drawn out "S-i-x-t-e-e-n..."

"Please, Jess! I'm sorry I called you a bitch, just—"

"Why? I *am* a bitch, honey. Seventeen," she added.

Autumn whimpered. "They're almost here." *Please don't look up, please don't look up.*

Jess let her off the hook. "Eighteen-Nineteen-*Twenty*," she rattled off quickly.

"Thank you," Autumn gasped as she propelled herself away from the window, tucking her tits back into the dress and not daring to look outside to determine whether she'd been seen.

"Your turn."

Autumn needed a moment as her heartbeat returned to normal. She took a breath. "Truth or Dare. Naughtiest thing you've ever done."

Jess pondered it. "A few years ago. I was at a *boring* wedding reception. Stepped out of the banquet hall to get some fresh air. In a smaller room, there was a bachelor party going on. Rather rowdy. And rather cute guys. I crashed."

"And?"

"They hadn't hired any, um, *entertainment*. I decided to remedy that."

Autumn gasped in horrified fascination. "You mean...?"

Jess giggled.

"I gave two BJs, including the groom to be. And danced topless. And they *all* were fondling me."

"Jess!"

"I was *totally* down with it. And—"

"Goodness. There's *more?*" Autumn asked, incredulous.

"There was another gal there. Girlfriend of one of the groomsmen. Very clingy type, wouldn't 'allow' him to go unless she tagged along." Jessica laughed wistfully. "She was *wasted*. I sixty-nined her on the table while the groom and his friends watched."

Briefly, Autumn recalled the time she'd fantasized about being in the same position with Jessica — the night she'd watched the porn movie.

"Damn!"

"Same question, Autumn. Naughtiest thing you've ever done."

"We're doing it right now," Autumn responded without missing a beat.

"Awwww. That's the sweetest thing anyone's ever said to me! I just might cry! Or come."

"Okay, okay." She searched for another question. "Truth or Dare. The night you called my number by mistake. Who were you really calling?"

"Who said it was by mistake, Autumn?" Jess asked quietly.

"But... But... How would you have gotten my—"

"Nah, I'm just kidding. I wasn't stalking you or anything like that." She cleared her throat. "I was trying to reach another friend. She'd changed her number, and I hadn't put the new one in my phone."

"Another friend..." All at once, Autumn was feeling fiercely jealous. "Is it someone you're... like... still..."

"Sorry," Jess informed reproachfully. "You can't ask two questions. My turn!" She came up with the next question. "Ever been restrained? Like, tied up? Handcuffed?"

"No," Autumn said, still very much distracted about Jessica's "another friend" answer. "Well, at most, once in a while, I've had a guy hold my wrists down while he's on top of me."

"Mmm, I *love* that."

Has this "another friend" done that for her?

"Next question?"

"Truth... or Dare." Autumn tried to keep her voice even and nonchalant, although she was more anxious than she'd care to admit. "Is this... other friend... someone you're, like, seeing? Involved with, meaning, like... you know..."

Jess tittered softly. "Dare."

The bitch. She knew she'd struck a chord and was playing on it. Autumn shook it off.

"Okay. The other day, you left me a message, where you, um, faked like you were... having..."

"An orgasm?" Jess offered helpfully.

"Uh, yeah." Autumn drank. "Your dare is to go open your window and, um, fake one, right now."

"*Oooooooh!* Autumn, you naughty *girl!*" Jess giggled good-naturedly. "Does it have to be a fake one? Because, well, I'm pretty much ready to go as it is..."

"Go to it."

Autumn heard her friend getting up, then the sound of the window opening.

"Do I have to stand in the window?"

"Near it."

Jess snorted.

"Hey, at least *you* aren't topless."

"You sure about that?"

Actually, she wasn't at all. Autumn was discovering that her friend was rather uninhibited.

"Ohhhhhhh. Autumn. Touch me..."

"You don't *have* to say my name," Autumn pointed out quickly. "Just the... uh, noises would be—"

"But what if I *want* to? Are you saying I *can't* say your name?"

"Yes. Uh, no. I mean... well, say whatever you... well, want to..." Autumn stammered, cursing herself silently. The point of the Dare had been to fluster Jess, not herself.

"Autumn... oh my God, I love it. Get your tongue on me. Oooooooooh yeah... ohhhhhh! Right... fucking... *there*... *yes*... *yessss*... *YES!!!!!* Yes, baby, *fuck me!*" Jess devolved into a series of blissful shrieks, and now Autumn couldn't tell if her phone friend was faking it or not.

In any case, her own hand had trailed down between her thighs, and *she* certainly wasn't faking her enjoyment at this point.

"How was that? Good enough?"

Autumn barely heard over the sound of her own heavy breathing and soft moaning.

"Oh, my. And are *you* faking it, Autumn?"

She pulled her hand away. "Oh. Sorry," she murmured sheepishly.

"How wet are you right now, compared to during one of your *other* dates?" Jess paused for a beat, then added, "That was your next question, by the way. Truth or Dare."

"Who says I'm... uh, wet?"

"Are you saying you're not? Because I think that would be lying."

"I'm, well, enjoying what we're—"

"Yes, but how much are you *enjoying*? How wet, compared to your other dates?"

Nobody, male or female, had *ever* invoked this sort of excitement in Autumn — until now. The answer, were she to give one, would involve some sort of comparison between a rainforest in Brazil and the Sahara Desert. But she wasn't quite ready to admit this to someone she had technically never met.

And, she couldn't envision herself lying to Jess. Ever.

"D-dare."

"This is going to be fun."

Autumn gulped, her pulse quickening as she waited for her next challenge.

"Do you have a measuring cup?"

"Well, sure, of course." Autumn fished the Pyrex cup out of her cabinet while wondering where her friend might be going with this.

Or, as it turned out, where Autumn herself would be going. "Now. Go to a neighbor's and ask to borrow a cup of sugar. In your best 'girl next door' voice."

"Like, a guy neighbor?"

"It can be another woman if you *want*. But I thought you were *straight*?"

"I am," Autumn said, although not nearly as convincingly as when she and Jess had started talking. "Okay, I should change clothes, I'm still in my—"

"No." Jessica was matter-of-fact, her tone final. "As you are."

"At least a bra." *Or panties*. Having planned on "getting lucky" that night, she'd gone without those as well.

"Nope."

"A cup of sugar? Kind of cliché, don't ya think?"

"Very."

She held up the Pyrex cup by its handle, studying the red measurement markings. "This cup is actually for liquid measurement. I'm not sure if I have one that—"

"Quit stalling, Autumn," her friend scolded good-naturedly. "And stay on the phone."

"Okay, okay." She didn't bother with her shoes, as the hallways in her apartment building were carpeted.

The guy down in 102 seemed "safe" for her Dare. They'd exchanged pleasantries and banter in the entryway and laundry room on a few occasions, and she'd once brought his mail to him when she'd gotten it by mistake. So, she made her way to the stairwell, measuring cup in one hand, phone against her ear with the other.

"Okay. I'm going downstairs. I can't believe I'm doing this..."

"You're doing great. Bet you're looking sexy."

"It's a nice dress."

"I'm sure it's more than just the dress. Now, remember, girl next door."

"Yes, I know, Jessica." She made it to the bottom landing. "I'll probably put the phone down when I—"

"Oh, that's right. You don't have a Bluetooth."

"Nope. Sheltered, remember?" She was coming to apartment 102. "Okay. Now keep quiet."

"Or maybe I'll get loud." She launched into another mini-performance of sultry moaning and cries of pleasure.

"Jess! Hush!"

"No fun," her friend pouted. Moving the cup to her other hand, Autumn hesitantly knocked on the door, fidgeting nervously.

Footsteps within the apartment, coming toward the door. It opened, and her neighbor answered. Her eyes swept over him—he was wearing baseball pants and an Under Armour shirt. He played for the local minor-league baseball team, she now remembered. He'd probably recently gotten home from practice and was now "unwinding." Briefly, Autumn wondered why she'd never gone on a date with *him*. She could do much worse. *And I have, this past couple of weeks,* she reminded herself.

"Hi. Can I help you...?"

"I'm Autumn. I live upstairs."

"Oh. I'm Jeff." He, in turn, was now checking *her* out.

Remembering her "mission," she bit her lip, fluttering her eyelashes at him. "Jeff, I *hate* to trouble you. But I was wondering if I could borrow a cup of sugar?" She willed herself not to laugh as she delivered the corny line, twisting her inevitable smirk into something more coy and suggestive.

His eyes took in her chest—the dress did a pretty decent job of putting her on display. *Although not like the "display" the people in the courtyard probably got,* she reminded herself.

"Baking tonight?"

"Yep." She met his eyes demurely, speaking a little louder than usual for Jessica's benefit. "Bored, alone on a Friday night... so, I'm baking."

A thought occurred to her. *What if he invites me in? And, offers to help me with my boredom? What do I do about the phone call?*

But he didn't. "Just one cup?"

"Oh. Yeah." She handed the *Pyrex* measuring cup over, allowing her hand to brush against his while looking at him steadily. Autumn was flirting a bit more heavily than usual — some of it was thanks to the healthy buzz from the vodka — but to an extent she was "showing off" for Jessica, whom she knew was listening intently.

"Just a minute." He took the proffered cup, shutting

the door part way and disappearing back into the apartment.

She raised the phone back to her ear. "Jess? Still there?"

"Still here," her friend murmured softly. "He sounds sexy. Is he hot?"

"He's... kinda cute..."

"Just 'kinda'? Don't hold out on me!"

"Well... he's a baseball player."

"*Oooooh!* An *athlete!* Sexy. Have you and he ever—"

"Gotta go, Jess, he's coming back." She took the phone away from her ear as the door opened again.

It wasn't Jeff. In the doorway stood a slender, rather pissed-off looking Hispanic woman of about twenty. In her hand, she clutched Autumn's measuring cup, now filled neatly to the one-cup hash mark with white sugar.

"A cup of sugar?" she asked sarcastically.

"Uh... yeah. I'm... uh, making a cake," she elaborated.

"I'm *sure* you are."

Jeff, now looking very sheepish and apologetic, appeared in the doorway slightly behind the woman.

"Anything *else* we can get you? Flour? A stick of butter, perhaps?" The woman glared disdainfully at Autumn's display of cleavage in the party dress. "A couple of eggs?"

"No."

"Are you *quite* sure?"

"No, just the... the sugar is fine." The angry woman handed the *Pyrex* cup over. Now flustered, Autumn tried to patch things up. "I don't think we've met? I'm, uh, Autumn. Your neighbor in 208."

"I'm Samantha. Jeff's *girlfriend*." Her eyes narrowed. "Well, 'Autumn in 208', there's a grocery store *right* down the block. The next time you're out looking for a *cup of sugar*."

The door slammed, followed by the woman's angry, raised voice as she laid into her boyfriend about his "visitor." Through the door, she heard something like "Is this one of Kelsi's little bimbos?"

Autumn barely made it back to the stairwell before she found herself doubled over in laughter. Bringing the phone back to her ear, she found that Jessica was pretty much doing the same.

"She was *pissed*," Autumn giggled. "Oh my God..."

"She's not going to come kick your ass, or anything, is she?"

"I can take care of myself." Still laughing near-hysterically, she hurried back to the safety of her apartment, taking care not to spill the precious cup of sugar.

"Sorry! That was funny as hell!"

"Yeah, but I'll probably have to deal with her in the hallway, or in the laundry room!"

"Yeah, that could be a problem." Jess gave her the perfect excuse. "Just explain to her that you're not into guys!"

"Sure. That will go over well." Autumn began rummaging through her cabinets.

"What are you up to now?"

"Well," Autumn explained, "since you made me go get a cup of sugar, I suppose I might as well bake a cake!"

"Yum, good thinking. I just sent out for pizza myself. Drinking on an empty stomach isn't a good idea."

They continued to play the game, exchanging naughty exposés about dating encounters, raunchy experiences, and sex toys, highlighted by a heated "debate" about whether Autumn's shower massager met the definition of a "sex toy." That conversation, in particular, had her blushing beet red.

After she got the cake into the oven, followed by a heavy helping of vodka, Autumn screwed up her courage and asked the question that had been on her mind for some time.

"Do you live nearby?"

Jess laughed. "Define 'nearby'."

"Well, your number shows up as 'unknown'. I don't know if you're in the same city, or, like, on the other side of the country."

"And why do you want to know?" Jessica pressed.

"Just to know. No big deal, just…"

"Hoping to meet me?"

"I don't know. Just curious, and was wondering ab—"

"Dare."

The bitch! She was doing this deliberately — certainly, she'd picked up on the fact that Autumn wanted to know, so she was purposely evading.

Fine. You want it, you got it.

"Ok, Jessica—"

"Hold that thought, sweetie. I think my pizza's here."

"Wait!" Autumn's emphatic response surprised even herself.

"Yes, dear?"

"I want you to… uh…"

"You want me to, what?" asked Jess, amused.

"I want you to… answer the door naked."

Now it was Jessica's turn to be shocked. "Autumn!"

"That's my name."

"You know I can't just—"

"Yes, you can," Autumn persisted. "If I can flash my tits at all my neighbors, and almost get my ass kicked for being a homewrecker..." She chuckled. "Get naked, Jessica."

"Okay, I'll answer... well, I'll answer *part* of your question, I—"

But Autumn wasn't buying. "Nope. You can't just change your mind. A Dare is a Dare."

"You're *really* gonna make me..." In the background of the phone call, Autumn heard the sound of an insistent doorbell. "Can I, like, at least put on a robe—"

"Nope." Savoring the moment, Autumn added, "Quit stalling!"

"*Bitch.*"

"Uh huh."

"Autumn..."

"Hurry up and answer the door," she teased. "I'm *starved*!"

"Okay. A Dare is a Dare?"

"Yup."

She could hear the rustling of Jess removing her clothing. The doorbell rang once more.

"Be right there," Jess yelled. The phone picked it up rather loudly, and Autumn momentarily took the phone away from her ear.

A deep breath. "Okay..."

"What are you wearing, Jess?"

"Not a thing. Except my Bluetooth."

"Ah. Gotta get me one of those, I guess?"

"Oh, yes," Jess replied sweetly. "Considering all the things I'm going to be making you do with your hands."

This sent a jolt through Autumn, contemplating what her friend might have in store for her.

"Okay. Here goes nothing."

Autumn's heart was pounding as she listened. She could only imagine how it must be for her friend. Completely naked, about to answer the door for a stranger.

I hope she doesn't get assaulted or something, because of me and some silly Truth or Dare game. Suddenly concerned, she contemplated telling Jessica to call it off and get dressed. But something told her that her friend, too, could take care of herself.

"Almost there," Jessica giggled nervously. "Can't believe I'm doing this."

The sound of a deadbolt being disengaged, and a door swinging open.

"Delivery for Jessica?" came a male voice from the background.

"That's me."

In her mind's eye, she could see her friend opening the door just a crack, peeking out from behind. The delivery guy, still unaware that anything was amiss, reading from his receipt.

"One pizza, sausage and extra cheese..."

She could hear the door swinging open, coupled with her friend breathing a little heavier in anticipation. Autumn envisioned the pizza boy, still checking the order over, probably not realizing his customer wasn't wearing a stitch of clothing. Not yet, but soon, very soon.

Jessica gave a very low but nervous giggle. At the same time, the pizza guy gasped, loud enough Autumn heard it easily. *Yep, he noticed.*

As it turned out, she needn't have worried about Jess falling prey to any untoward behavior. Instead, the delivery boy all at once turned ultra-polite. "A-and, um, a side of, um, breadsticks, ma'am." Autumn could picture him now. Nervously fumbling with the order, struggling to maintain eye contact with so much else to look at. Hadn't Jessica mentioned having "double-Ds"?

"Do you have marinara sauce?" Although Jess must have been extremely nervous, she sounded like her usual self. Confident, flirty, and sexy.

"Y-yes ma'am. I, um, even, here's some extra, and no charge."

"It was warm," Jessica explained. No doubt, her pizza

guy was staring at her, probably with his mouth agape, wondering why she'd answered the door stark naked. "It's a *little* cooler now. Obviously," she finished with a playful giggle. It took Autumn a moment to unravel that one, but she finally got it. Jessica's nipples were hard.

That poor pizza guy. Autumn giggled at the thought.

"That's... well... nineteen f-fifty, ma'am."

"Oh," Jessica purred, "I forgot my purse. Be right back."

"Y-yes, ma'am."

The low, sexy laugh again. "Still there, Autumn?"

"Yes," she whispered excitedly.

"He's checking out my ass now."

"I'll bet it's lovely, Jess."

"Never had any complaints. And certainly not hearing any now."

"Are you okay?"

"Oh God, Autumn, I'm so fucking turned on."

Autumn simply couldn't help herself. "Gonna give him a special tip?"

"Mmm. You never know."

Jess rummaged around, and a few moments later Autumn heard her walking back toward her "guest."

"Miss me?"

"Uh, yes, ma'am."

I wish I were there, Autumn thought.

"Here's twenty-five. Keep the change, hon."

"Thank you... Ma'am, are you okay? Do you... uh, want some company, maybe?"

"Sorry, I kinda have other plans tonight!" But then, at the end came the sound of a kiss — *a smack on the cheek, not like the kiss she might give me.*

"Gotta go enjoy my pizza. Nite!" And then, the sound of the door being closed.

"Oh, fuck, Autumn, that was *so* hot!"

"Sounds like it," Autumn panted, her breathing now

somewhat labored. She'd been very turned on throughout Jessica's exhibitionist Dare. But now that she was sure her friend was safe, she felt able to relax and let herself go. Her fingers were already working their magic quite well.

"Sounds like things are hot over there as well!"

She groaned an emphatic *yes* while continuing to touch herself.

"Maybe you'd better get naked too, Autumn."

"On it." In nothing flat, the dress was on its way to the floor.

"Good."

"Not good," corrected Autumn, burying two fingers in her pussy now. "Fucking *wonderful*."

"*Mmm*." Jessica moaned softly as she began pleasuring herself. Autumn, on the other hand, was nearly already "there," but slowed her tempo and backed off at the last possible moment. Once again tonight, she gathered, Jess had some "catching up" to do.

"Fuck, that was great, Autumn."

Autumn blissfully murmured her agreement. She'd counted three orgasms and had listened to Jess reel off at least four. It was safe to say the disastrous "no-show" date earlier tonight was all but forgotten.

"I just thought of something."

Dreamily, her voice far away, Jess responded. "What's that, honey?"

"Well... who won the game?"

"Truth or Dare? Seems to me like we both came out on top."

"It was awesome," Autumn acknowledged. "I'm really comfortable talking to you."

Loud laughter. "Well, I would certainly hope so! Considering."

Autumn joined in, laughing as well.

"I'm glad. Comfortable with you, too, Autumn."

There was a long but very serene pause.

"Falling asleep over here. *Mmm*. Satisfaction."

"I feel you." Jess sighed. "Yeah... I guess it's time to get to bed. Sweet dreams, love."

"Good night. Sweet dreams."

She set the phone on her nightstand. Two minutes later, it announced an *UNKNOWN CALLER* again.

"Miss me already, Jess?"

"The 'other friend' you wanted to know about. Her name is Amber. I knew her when we were growing up. She lives far away, but we still talk once in a while. Sometimes gets pretty raunchy, but nothing has ever 'gone on' with her. And never will."

"Aw, Jessica. You didn't have to explain. You don't owe—"

"I wanted to."

Autumn grinned. "Well, thank you." She paused, thinking back on the questions *she'd* dodged tonight, then went on. "Jess... I said your name quite a few times. Screamed it." She giggled. "Once, I even had to shove a pillow over my face to keep myself quiet."

"Really?"

"Yes. Really." Naughtily, she told Jessica of the time she'd fucked her vibrator, coming so hard and so loudly a neighbor had beaten on the wall to urge her to keep it down. "Come to think of it, it was probably that woman downstairs. The one with the cup of sugar."

"Probably. It's a small world."

That got Autumn wondering again, about Jessica's proximity. "How small, exactly?"

"Good night, Autumn."

Jessica called a few times over the weekend. Autumn found herself to be somewhat standoffish and "guarded," feeling a bit awkward after the raunchy, intimate conversation with her phone friend. Jess seemed to be understanding of this, giving space as needed. Both girls steered somewhat clear of much of the subject matter they'd explored during Truth or Dare night, with one exception. Autumn had become determined to figure out where her friend was.

Later Sunday evening, the familiar *UNKNOWN CALLER* alert.

"H'lo?"

"Did I wake you?"

"Yeah. I must have dozed off."

"Sorry..."

"Oh, no, I still have to get some things ready for tomorrow. It's cool." She paused. "What time is it?"

"It's about eleven thirty. Eastern time." Autumn could hear the underlying mirth in her friend's voice.

"What about local time?"

"It probably says it on your phone," Jess said, quietly smug.

Bitch.

"What are you up to this week?"

"Work. And more work."

"Anything fun? More blind dates?"

"Probably. I'm a glutton for punishment like that." Autumn pondered for a moment. "There's one guy I've seen a few times. Maybe doing something with him Friday. It's my birthday, so maybe I'll treat myself to more than another God-awful first date."

"Ooooooh. Birthday..." A thoughtful pause. "Good, that gives me enough time to work on a gift for you."

"A gift? What kind?"

"A surprise."

"Like what?"

"It's a surprise!"

Autumn smiled. "Is it you?" she asked, half-jokingly.

"Hmm... yes and no."

"What do you mean, yes and no? You don't even know what it is. You just found out about my birthday five seconds ago!"

"I work fast."

"Mmm hmm. That you do." Autumn laughed. "But you don't *have* to get me anything!"

"I want to."

Well, if she sends me something, reasoned Autumn, *I'll be able to tell where it comes from.* The "Jessica mystery" had been driving her nuts — a fact which obviously hadn't escaped her mysterious friend, who seemed to use it to tease Autumn at every opportunity.

"So, do you need my address?" she asked innocently.

"Nope."

"Then, how would you—"

"Whew, look at the time! I've got lots to do, Friday is going to be here quickly!"

"Jess! Aren't you going to give me a *hint*?"

"Not yet. I gotta get going — unless you're gonna help me rub one out?"

Autumn giggled, blushing a little. "I'll take a rain check." *Aw, c'mon, Autumn, you know you're going to do it anyway once she hangs up.*

"Okay, can't blame a gal for trying. Sweet dreams, Autumn."

Tuesday. Another lousy first/last date. Like clockwork, Autumn's smartphone went off just as she took the first customary swig of vodka.

"Whatcha doing?"

"Just home early from another date."

"How was this one?"

"About the usual." She took another drink.

"In love with his car?"

"Nah."

"Mommy fixation? Porn addiction?"

"Nope."

"Premature ejaculation?"

Autumn giggled. "No!"

"If it comes to that, I've got a whole suitcase full of fun things that never go soft. Just saying."

"Nice to know, Jess." She laughed. "So, we emailed

one another and had planned to go out to eat. I suggested Olive Garden. And, supposedly because I named the place, *I* became fully responsible for the check!"

"Like... all of it?"

"All of it. No going Dutch, no nothing. Another one for the trash folder."

"Three more days."

"Yep. Three more days." Autumn wondered if her friend had been serious about giving her some form of gift for her birthday.

"Any fun plans yet?"

"I have the day off. I figured I'd pamper myself a little."

"No date?"

"There's this one guy who's halfway decent. We're going out to dinner."

"Is he gonna get lucky?"

"To hell with that, it's my day. Aren't *I* supposed to be the one getting lucky?"

"Mmm, I sure hope so."

"How's your week going? What have you been up to?"

"Going okay. Working on a special little project. For someone special."

"Oh yeah? How's that going?"

"Coming along nicely. We'll know soon."

"Will we, now."

"What kind of vodka are we having tonight?"

"This one's whipped cream flavored."

"Ooooooooh. Can't go wrong with whipped cream, can we?"

"No." Autumn smiled. "I guess we can't."

"So... are you drunk enough for me to take advantage of you yet?"

A laugh. "Not yet. I'm going easy on it. Early day tomorrow."

"Damn," Jessica sighed. "Guess it's the Energizer bunny tonight."

The two girls bantered a little more, and then ended the call and headed to bed.

Friday morning. Eight twenty a.m. Taking advantage of her day off, Autumn slept in, although just a bit. *Happy birthday to me.*

She checked the phone and did a double-take. "*10 New Messages*".

"Damn, Jess. *Someone* wants to talk to me," she murmured, amused.

After brushing her teeth and showering, she grabbed the phone again and checked the first message.

"Happy birthday, Autumn. I promised you a gift today. It's at Southfield Mall. Don't play the next voicemail till you get there. Have fun, sweetie!"

Autumn swallowed, her heart racing. *A gift?* The mall was across town, about forty minutes away in good traffic. But this must mean her "mystery friend" was indeed local?

Will she be there?

All at once, she began primping herself, as if she were a young girl about to encounter her crush.

That's not too far from the truth, is it, Autumn?

"She's just a friend," she reminded the flustered-looking young woman in the mirror. *She probably sent some gift certificate for me to pick up.*

Nevertheless, she hit herself up with her lilac body spray before shrugging into her grey-trim, knit cami and her cropped jeggings. Ten minutes later, she was in her car and pulling out of the apartment complex parking lot.

Before she made it two blocks, however, her curiosity got the better of her, and she clicked on the second message.

"Hey, birthday girl. Have I piqued your *curiosity*?"

"Well, yes," Autumn admitted as her friend's voice paused.

"Well, you're a very *bad* girl, Autumn. Your instructions were to *not* listen to the next message till you got to the mall! *Shame* on you. Your disobedience will certainly be addressed later!" The message ended.

Autumn grinned, putting the phone away as she hurried in the direction of the mall.

She parked outside the main entrance, exited the car, and locked it with her key fob over her shoulder. Her eyes skimmed the parking lot and the multiple glass doors ahead of her.

Is she here? Is she watching? Autumn felt a thrill at the possibility.

People were coming and going, but nobody who would seem to match the profile of her "special friend."

Not that you have any idea what she looks like.

Taking a deep breath, Autumn stepped onto the sidewalk and strode beneath the SOUTHFIELD MALL lettering toward the multiple glass doors and into the shopping center.

The mall was divided into three levels with this being the Main. A display board with a lighted map showed the store directory by levels, and beyond that, a square common area flanked by benches. On one of these sat a tall brunette in a blue sweater.

Could that be Jessica? Autumn eyed the young woman nonchalantly as she stepped up to the directory and pretended to study it. But a moment later, the woman's smartphone went off.

"Hello? Yeah. I'll be out there in about an hour." The woman's voice had a heavy Bronx accent — plus, she was paying no attention whatsoever to anyone coming or going. Definitely not Jess.

So, what now?

She stood perplexed for a moment, until she recalled the eight messages waiting on her phone. With another look around, trying to figure out if her "phone friend" was watching from somewhere, she clicked the next message and put the phone to her ear.

"I guess you're at the mall now? Hope you didn't have any trouble finding the place!" A self-assured giggle. "You should go treat yourself to a cup of coffee. And be sure to tell the barista it's your birthday!"

Frowning, she checked the phone. That was the extent of the message. *Nothing about* where *exactly I'm supposed to go.*

Was there supposed to be more? Should she go to the

next message?

She checked the directory board again. Under the *Specialty Food* heading, there was only one coffee-related listing: STARBUCKS — K17. The "K" indicated a kiosk, which the map identified as being here on the main level. Autumn headed that way.

At the handful of tables near the Starbucks booth, a few people were sipping various coffee drinks. She looked them over. One man and four women. None of these seemed to be Jessica either — *she mentioned having big boobs,* Autumn reminded herself.

Besides, she wouldn't really know when *I was coming.*

The barista's name was Angie, so *this* wasn't her either — unless "Jessica" was a made-up name. Autumn found this unlikely, however.

"What'll you have, hon?" Angie was waiting patiently on her.

"Oh. Sorry." Her eyes studied the board behind the counter. "A tall latte, please."

"Name?"

"Autumn." She handed over her credit card, taking a moment to scan the display case containing the various cookies and pastries.

"Can I get you something from there?"

Autumn grinned. "I *should*. It's my birthday, maybe I should treat my—"

"Oh!" Angie brightened. "You're *Autumn!*"

"Yes, I am." Autumn smiled, a little confused.

"One moment!" The barista handed the credit card back. "Need your receipt?"

"No, I'm good."

Angie went to work making her drink, and Autumn returned to scrutinizing the mall, looking for any sign of Jessica.

"Latte for Autumn!"

She stepped to the pick-up area, expecting the white cup with her name scrawled on it in Sharpie. Instead, Angie was holding a black ceramic tumbler, adorned with red and white hearts plus the familiar green mermaid logo.

"Oh, I didn't order—"

"The cup is a gift for you," Angie explained. "Happy birthday!"

"Thank you!" Shrugging, she took a sip of her drink. "Who left this for me?" Although she knew who, she nevertheless seized upon the opportunity to glean more info about her friend.

"All I know is that there was a note when I started. It said that someone named Autumn would be stopping by, and that it was your birthday!" The grin playing at Angie's lips suggested she knew a little more than she was telling, but Autumn didn't press the matter.

So, she was here.

Or, maybe Jess was indeed thousands of miles away and had just arranged the gift over the phone.

Enjoy it, Autumn, she chided herself. *Whether she's peeking around the corner or on the other side of the country, she took the time to get you something really nice.*

She took a seat. While she enjoyed the latte, Autumn went back to her phone. She'd followed the instructions in the last voicemail, so it would be okay to listen to the next one, wouldn't it?

She shrugged, clicking.

"Hey, sweetie. Now that you've had your coffee, sit down and relax while you look for *solutions*."

Autumn's brow furrowed as she frowned thoughtfully. "Solutions to what?"

She kept looking around the mall. Still, just normal shopper activity. Above her, on the upper level, nobody peering studiously down upon her. Here on the Main, just the standard fare of shops, again with nothing or nobody out of the ordinary. The Starbucks was flanked by a few other kiosks: one selling cell phones and accessories, the other featuring knock-off colognes and perfumes. Both shops, however, were staffed by young men.

What am I supposed to be solving?

She took another look in the direction of the phone kiosk, and suddenly made the connection. Cellular Solutions, the sign at the top of the booth proclaimed.

Okay, Jess, I got your clue. Now what?

Taking her tumbler, she walked toward the booth. The young clerk engaged her while she was still a dozen steps away. These cell phone salespeople at the mall were *very* pushy, she knew from experience.

"Good morning. May I ask who you're using for your phone provider?"

"Hi. This may sound strange, but..." Autumn took a deep breath. "Has anyone... left any kind of message, or anything, for me?"

"What's your name?"

"Autumn."

The salesman brightened. "Just a minute." He retreated into his kiosk, digging out a plastic shopping bag from beneath the counter. A Post-It note on the front of the bag announced that this was for *AUTUMN — she will pick up today!*

"Thanks."

"You're welcome. Can I interest you in—"

"No, thanks, I'm covered." She held up her phone. "Just got a new plan. I'm stuck for two years." *A little white lie never hurt anyone.*

Autumn returned to her seat at Starbucks. The Cellular Solutions guy was already engaged in selling another prospective customer. She opened the plastic bag to find a small gift-wrapped package.

Jess wrapped this herself. For some reason, she was sure of it. Her hands trembled slightly as her fingers fumbled with the wrapping. When she saw the contents, she smiled. It was a Bluetooth headset.

There was also a folded note, written in neat, flowery penmanship: *Now your hands can be free... like mine! Happy birthday!* There was a smiley face and a heart drawn on the note.

She kept sipping her coffee as she thumbed through the instruction book for the Bluetooth. It was a small square booklet with instructions in five different languages, which meant there wasn't very much to it. She addressed the section entitled "Pairing", accessing the corresponding settings on her smartphone until she was rewarded with a blue light on the earpiece.

Autumn put the Bluetooth on her ear, then selected

the voicemail message she'd already listened to. In her ear, Jessica's sweet voice instructed her again to look for "solutions."

"Thanks, Jess," she said aloud. She was now feeling a bit guilty, though. The Bluetooth headset was a nice one, very "high-end", and the Starbucks cup couldn't have been cheap either. Plus, there were still seven voicemail messages left — presumably, each corresponding to a gift. *How much did you spend on my birthday? You didn't have to!*

In her mind, she could hear that sweet, low voice, *But I wanted to, Autumn.*

She was slightly misty-eyed while she finished off the rest of her coffee.

Autumn grabbed a few napkins and wiped the tumbler dry, inside and out. Carefully, she tucked it into the bag she'd gotten from the cellular shop and went to the next voicemail. A few seconds later, Jessica's wonderful voice was in her ear.

"Now that your hands are going to be free, let's give you something to do with them!" Jessica giggled. "There was this store that seemed *really* exciting. Until I found out that they don't carry schoolgirl skirts, nurse outfits, or cops' and robbers' uniforms. Although, I think you might bump into some of your first dates there! So, you'll probably want to go next door instead. Just follow the techno music!"

Autumn had to play this one back a few times, and even then, she didn't get it. *A uniform store, maybe?*

Perplexed, she walked back to the mall directory and perused it. If she recalled correctly, at one time there had been a clothing store for expectant mothers, which had included work uniforms and attire. It had been either Working Mothers or Mother's Work — but it didn't seem to be on the directory anymore. Nor was there anything else pertaining to uniforms or such clothing. *So much for that.*

She retraced her steps back to the coffee kiosk, looking around the mall for anything that might give her a clue.

Let's see, she mused, *if I were a slightly off-my-rocker woman walking the mall, where would I go?*

Immediately on the heels of that, she got angry at

herself for thinking that. *If any of these jerks you date were half as thoughtful as Jessica, you'd be living happily ever after.*

She played the message again, this time while walking the mall. At the part about the "techno music," she stopped, listening. She heard the normal bustle of the mall, plus the occasional *ding* of the elevator at the center atrium. And now, faintly, she *could* hear music. Techno or not, it had bass, and seemed to carry through the mall. It was definitely coming from the direction in which she was heading.

She passed Foot Locker, Lids (wasn't that one owned by Foot Locker as well?) and a bookstore, and as she rounded a bend in the mall's layout, she found the source of the music. Spencer's, an adult-geared gift and novelty store.

It could be? As she got closer, the music coming from the store changed to another upbeat number — definitely "techno." She pondered the clue she'd been given, also looking around at the other shops at this end of the mall. Right next to the gift store was an RPG and fantasy shop called RolePlay Universe.

Now it clicked. "Roleplay" she knew, was also a term

for sexual play in which the participants might dress up — *like as a schoolgirl, police officer, or nurse*, she thought excitedly. Someone seeing the name *might*, therefore, assume that RolePlay Universe referred to sexy dress-up — until they got inside and looked around.

Wait! The comparison to the guys I date. Jess, you bitch! Autumn cursed her friend — until she saw a couple of geekish thirty-something guys walking out of the store, D&D purchases in hand. *Sheesh, she's right. In fact, these people would be an* improvement *over my dating life.*

Autumn was now confident that she'd unraveled the riddle — i.e. the store *next* to RolePlay Universe with the techno beat being pumped out. *Thank goodness, she left that clue — I would have wandered the mall all day without figuring out the RPG part.*

Her heartbeat quickened as she entered Spencer's. The clerk was a very short, rather full-figured young woman who couldn't have been more than nineteen. Her Spencer's nametag identified her as *CASEY*. Aside from her smock, she was clad in all black with matching lipstick, had violet hair and numerous piercings — Autumn counted seven. *And those are just the ones that are visible.*

As she approached, Casey eyed her, looking bored and chomping away at a piece of bubblegum.

Sheepishly, Autumn spoke. "Hi. Is there... something left here for me?"

"Are you Autumn?" Casey asked immediately.

"Uh, yeah."

"Here ya go." Casey handed over not one, but two gift-wrapped packages.

"Thanks." Autumn smiled. "Hey, did you by any chance see who dropped this off?"

The clerk steadily chomped at her gum. "Uh huh."

Autumn's eyes lit up excitedly. "Really? Can you tell me about her?"

"Uh-uh." When Autumn raised an eyebrow, Casey elaborated on this. "Confidentiality. H.H.P.A. laws and all that, you know."

"What?" Autumn looked at the clerk, agape. "Do you mean HIPAA?"

"I prefer the term *curvy*, thank you very much," Casey

snapped.

"No," said Autumn quickly. "*HIPAA* is a law, but... it's just that it applies to doctors, not to—"

"You gonna buy anything?"

"Just, uh, picking up these." Autumn held up the two gifts, wondering how she'd gotten into this conversation. Quickly, she made her exit as Casey watched her go. She looked around for a place to open her new gifts, settling on a more secluded bench. The items from this particular store could be rather risqué and might be embarrassing to open in front of other people.

As it turned out, this was a wise decision. The first gift was a Best Weekend Ever Sex Kit, and it contained several unmentionable items that immediately turned Autumn's face bright red. It included two vibrators, a tickler, and a sexy eye mask. There was also another folded note from Jess. "*If you need someone to demonstrate any of these, don't hesitate to ask! Happy birthday, sweetie!*" Again, the note was adorned with hearts and smileys.

She put the kit safely into her bag, looked again and fumbled with the wrapping of the second item.

This one was a pinkish book/box. The front was titled *COSMO'S TRUTH OR DARE: Our Naughtiest Sex Game Ever!* Inside were a number of tear-out cards, each with a "truth" question and a "dare" challenge. Again, there was a note.

"I think we covered some of these already! Can't wait to play again! Love, Jess"

Autumn smiled wistfully as she recalled the incredibly erotic evening on the phone. She was still blushing hotly and took another look around to make sure nobody had observed her with the naughty gifts. Once more, she wondered if Jessica might be somewhere in the mall, watching from a distance. *And waiting to pounce?* The thought made her quiver.

She added the naughty game, and Jessica's note, to the bag, and queued up the next voicemail.

"I'll bet nobody at that mall knows what a *bad* girl you are, Autumn!" The melodious giggle again. "Talking to strangers on the phone... the naughty things that happen in your shower... too bad I know *all* about them!" Jess took a breath and continued in a "pouty but stern" voice. "There's a bench right next to the 'up' escalator. Now go sit down, and give yourself a time out."

"And then what?" Autumn asked the mall at large. No answer was forthcoming, though. Following Jessica's instructions, she set off for the twin escalators, easily spotting the bench right next to the one leading to the upper level of the mall.

She took her seat, wondering if she was supposed to wait a certain amount of time? Or was there another clue here?

Am I supposed to go to the next message now? But Autumn didn't think so — thus far, each of the messages had led to a gift.

Autumn looked up, and smiled. Directly in front of her, not twenty feet away, was a shop: Time Out Liquor Store.

"Give yourself a time out." She laughed at her friend's clever play on words as she got to her feet.

By now, she was getting used to the drill. *Did someone leave something here for me?* and *did you see who left this?* This time, the clerk produced a small gift bag for her — pink, her favorite color — but before handing it over, he asked for her ID. This resulted in another "happy birthday" wish, which left Autumn doubly grateful. Now that she was a year older, it was getting to the point where being carded was a compliment.

The gift bag was stuffed with tissue paper in various shades of pink. Underneath were several miniature plastic bottles of vodka, in various flavors including peach, cranberry, wedding cake, and of course, pineapple and mango.

Jess, you certainly do *know me well*, Autumn smiled to herself. She blushed again as she checked the handwritten note. "*Because I want to get you drunk and take advantage of you...*"

"Oh, how sweet." She giggled.

On to the next clue. "Go up the escalator, and I'm sure you'll find the next *secret...*" This one was incredibly easy, and Autumn had it figured out while the escalator was still ascending — even before she saw the familiar posters of lingerie-clad models, and the big logo for the PINK line of products.

The Victoria's Secret salesgirl seemed to be ready for

her, producing the large pink shopping bag almost as soon as Autumn gave her name.

"Thank you."

"Happy birthday!"

This time, Autumn didn't try to "fish" for information about Jessica. If and when she wanted to reveal herself, she would. And in the meantime, the "scavenger hunt" had been a lot of fun.

She retreated to a bench on the upper level opposite VS, opening the bag and checking her "spoils." There was a long-sleeve red tee, cropped at the midriff and adorned with the words "PINK NATION", and gray "boyfriend pants" with "PINK" emblazoned on the seat. Out of curiosity, she checked the tag for the size, and her face flushed yet again. The attached tag was labeled PINK and BOYFRIEND PANTS, but Jess had drawn a line through "BOY" and scrawled "GIRL" beneath it. She looked up and noticed the salesgirl was watching her, smiling, and she offered a weak wave in return.

Quickly, she turned her attention back to the bag. There were a couple of other gifts included. A bath bomb and a bottle of Secret Garden Secret Crush Indulgent Bubbles.

Autumn's thoughts inevitably returned to *her* "secret crush." *Jess! You shouldn't have! This is so... wonderful.*

She again had to will herself not to get choked up. She looked up and down the mall for the umpteenth time, hoping her mysterious friend would show herself.

"I'd totally kiss you," she whispered aloud. "And... whatever you wanted..." She was shocked at her forwardness, even though it wasn't within earshot of anyone else.

The next message was vintage Jessica.

"Ready for your next surprise, Autumn? Next, you'll be going down..." Jessica's voice dropped to a silky whisper. "Wish it were on me." A flirty moan, and she continued. "All the way *down*... oh, Autumn... yes... right *there*... oooooh... ohhhh... *ohhhhh*..." At this point, Jess descended into about thirty seconds of orgasmic moaning, groaning, and screaming, with Autumn all the while wondering if her friend were faking it or really getting herself off.

Abruptly, Jessica's voice snapped back to normal. "Oh, sorry, where were we? Oh, yes. When you get off the elevator, take a right. Take sixty-nine steps. Ooooooh sixty-nine, baby, do me, and I'll do you! Oh, Autumn, *yes*!"

Autumn couldn't decide whether she was supposed to be amused or turned on. Right now, she was feeling quite a bit of both.

"On second thought, make it seventy-seven steps. It's your birthday, so it's only right that you should get 'ate more'." Momentary cackling at her own pun. "Is that okay with you, sweetie? Hope so, because I'm hungry." The lusty moaning started up again. "Well, you've got your clue," Jess said hastily. "Gotta go..." Her moans and yelps quickly grew in intensity, and the voicemail abruptly ended.

When Autumn played the message back a second time, she tried to tell herself it was *just* so that she could get the clues right.

The elevator was at the very center, where the three "legs" of the mall came together. Alone in the elevator, she studied the buttons.

"All the way down," she mused, pressing the button

for LL — Food Court. As the elevator began to descend, it agitated the butterflies in her stomach even more as she wondered what her friend might have in store next.

At the main level, the doors opened, and several other shoppers got in. When they reached the food court, she waited for everyone else, then stepped out of the elevator.

Sixty-nine steps. No, she said seventy-seven. Her arousal grew as she thought about Jessica's colorful joke.

She counted her steps, passing a few fast-food places including Panda Express, Mrs. Field's, and Harold's Chicken. Seventy-seven brought her in front of Cinnabon with its pastries beckoning her, calling to her from their glass display case.

Great, I hope you got me a gym membership too, Jess. She grinned, waiting for the server who was helping another customer. After a couple of mouth-watering minutes, it was her turn.

"Hi," she explained, "you *might* have something set aside for me?"

The girl stepped around to a baking area in the rear of the small store, grabbing a *Cinnabon* bag. "Are you

Autumn?"

"Yes, that's me." She took the bag, peering inside. Nestled in a teal cup was a very decadent-looking caramel-covered cinnamon roll. The picture marquee above the counter identified this particular delight as the Caramel PecanBon. In the center was a single pink candle. *Happy birthday to me.*

"Thank you," she told the clerk. "This looks absolutely delicious." After a moment's consideration, Autumn decided that she'd better add a box of cinnamon rolls, just in case.

By now, Autumn realized that her birthday "treasure hunt" would be drawing to a close — there were just a few messages left. Now, she was wondering more and more if Jess herself would be at the end of this "quest." Accordingly, she was super-nervous... and super-excited.

The next clue wasn't too difficult either. "Time to go back to the main level. Autumn, I sincerely hope I've done my part to make your birthday a *thing* to be *remembered*."

"You certainly have, Jessica," she announced to the empty elevator before stepping out and heading back in the direction of the mall entrance.

She spent a little time browsing around Southfield's Things Remembered shop, wanting her birthday excursion to last as long as possible. Finally, her curiosity got the better of her and she stepped up to the counter.

The clerk handed over a nondescript black box. Like the rest, she either had no information about the mysterious gift-giver or she'd been sworn to secrecy. With a *thank you*, Autumn returned to the mall and took a seat at the same Starbucks table where she'd begun. Eagerly, she lifted the lid of the black box. Inside was a Styrofoam insert with two cutout areas. One of these contained a custom-engraved shot glass, which she now took out and turned over between her fingers. One side had *Autumn* engraved in cursive, and the other side of the glass read "Great minds..."

The other cutout opening was empty, and Autumn guessed that Jess was in possession of the other shot glass. She also had a pretty good idea what was probably etched on it. *Now I'll have a glass to use next time Jess wants to make a toast. We both will.*

Out of the blue, she wondered if the two shot glasses

would ever be in the same place, to be clinked together in a toast by their respective "owners." The thought made her quiver all over.

Maybe that will happen now. Hey, I've got the vodka for it, Jess. You just bring... um... yourself.

There was only one message left on her phone. Autumn carefully laid the shot glass back in the box, preparing to close the lid — but then stopped. There was something rattling around at the bottom of the box, beneath the insert. Taking care not to break the Styrofoam, she pried it up and set it off to the side. In the box was an orange key with a numbered tag on it and an envelope. She opened the latter, examining its contents with a gasp of shocked delight.

In the envelope was a photo of the other shot glass in the set — snugly nestled between a pair of rather large but firm breasts. The picture — presumably of Jessica — had been cropped to call attention to the display. She was wearing a pink, silky robe, which was open and barely covered the wearer's nipples. Her upper chest was slightly freckled, and just above her left boob was the heart tattoo Jess had alluded to during the Truth or Dare game. At the top of the photo, a set of pink glossed lips were curled into an absolutely breathtaking *come-hither* smile, and a few locks of lovely red hair fell on her shoulders.

A redhead. Well, that explains it, she grinned to herself, although her eyes kept returning to the lovely set of breasts which were nearly swallowing up the shot glass. Just as she'd suspected, the other glass from the set was etched with the conclusion of the catch phrase: ". . .think alike!"

She ogled the photo for several minutes, studying every sexy detail. Her eyes returned to the tattoo. The heart was a darker red in places, and Autumn eventually realized that at some point, a "cover up" had been done — most likely to conceal a name.

She's had her heart broken. Suddenly, Autumn felt fiercely protective toward her friend. *Damn, why would anyone ever hurt you*, she wanted to ask Jess. *I hope you're here somewhere.*

The thought brought her back to the orange key. Maybe when she found whatever it opened, she'd find Jessica and meet her special friend face-to-face.

What if I want to kiss her? Their conversations (and

some of the items in today's treasure hunt) suggested that Jess was highly adventurous. But what if she didn't like Autumn in person? Jessica was sexy and beautiful, based upon the little bit she'd seen, but Autumn had always thought of herself as a "plain Jane". Boring and nondescript.

She held up the key, studied it. Autumn wasn't too surprised when she realized that the number on the tag was sixty-nine.

What does this go to? A locker?

After some exploration of the mall — now eyeing and carefully scrutinizing every female shopper or mall employee with red hair and big boobs — Autumn indeed found a side corridor beneath a MALL SERVICES sign. Halfway down was an area with a bank of storage lockers. She perused the numbers until she found sixty-nine. The locker door was slightly larger than a square foot. *Well, I'm sure Jess isn't waiting in there for me!*

Glancing back down the hallway as if she were doing something secretive, she stepped up to the locker and tried the key.

The locker clicked open. As is the case with most public lockers, there was a slightly dank, musty scent. She peered in, finding a regular box. Another note on the top merely announced, "From Me."

She took the box, double-checking to make sure nothing else was in the locker before closing it. Autumn made her way back out to the main mall, again, seeking out an out-of-the-way place to sit and open her gift. There were three items inside. An exquisitely gift-wrapped white package, an envelope, and a soft item wrapped in tissue paper — quite likely, more clothing.

She tore open the envelope first to find a gift card — for Olive Garden. An accompanying card read *"Treat yourself... you deserve it! Love, Jess."* Autumn smiled. Olive Garden was her absolute favorite, and Jessica had been thoughtful enough to pick up on that.

The tissue-wrapped gift was next. She tore the wrapping open at the seam, uncovering a silky, pink robe — the same one, she realized, as Jess had been wearing in the photo.

She wasn't wearing anything else when she wore this, Autumn reminded herself, and the thought made her feel incredibly aroused. As she held up the robe, another little note fell out. "Something of mine."

Clutching the robe, she caught the faint scent of perfume, and of freshly washed hair. Jessica's scent.

Autumn had a pretty good idea what she'd be wearing to bed tonight.

She'd saved the white box for last. It was from the San Francisco Music Box Company. Trembling with anticipation, she worked to undo the ribbon. *Oh, Jess, you got me something really beautiful*, she knew.

She removed the tissue from inside the box to reveal a lovely water globe with a beautiful red rose within. The base was wood-toned, and when she wound it, the globe played the familiar melody of "The Rose".

"Jess..." she whispered, now wiping tears away. "You're so beautiful." Passers-by were undoubtedly looking at her, but she didn't care at this point. The tune played for a few bars, until it needed to be wound again. *This is so beautiful.*

There was one more voice message now. Autumn adjusted her new Bluetooth earpiece, then clicked. Once more, Jessica's sweet, wispy voice filled her ear.

"I just want to wish you a happy birthday, Autumn. Today is a celebration of the day someone really wonderful was born!"

Thanks, Jess, because I wasn't crying enough already.

"I have to work today, a double shift again. So, I won't be off till late. After eleven. But I'll call you if that's ok. Because I do want to wish you happy birthday myself!"

"Sure thing, Jess." Autumn smiled through her tears, getting herself somewhat under control as she gathered up all the gifts she'd received on her treasure hunt. Part of her was disappointed Jessica hadn't been here in person. But, then again, the mystery about her was one of the many things that excited Autumn.

One of the many things I love about her.

Picking up her bags, she waved at a few of the bewildered shoppers who were looking her way, then strode toward the exit.

Idle hands do the devil's work. And, well, Autumn was certainly "idle." It was still hours before her birthday date with Chaz.

She spent some of it looking over the presents she'd gotten from Jessica. When she'd gotten home, she'd tried on the Victoria's Secret cropped tee and the PINK boyfriend pants. Correction: GIRLfriend pants. Both had fit very well, plus were extremely comfortable for lounging around the apartment as Autumn was doing today.

She found herself again checking out the photo Jessica had left her. The smile was hypnotizing. Jessica's pink glossed lips had that moist look to them, as if she'd just licked them. This, in turn, led to other thoughts. Jessica, licking her lips while sitting next to Autumn, coolly checking her out.

Jessica's tongue, meeting hers in a passionate, explosive kiss.

Jessica's tongue, licking other things...

Now, Autumn was getting aroused. She might have still been okay if her attention hadn't been drawn to the Best Weekend Ever Sex Kit and its array of naughty unmentionables. There were two vibrators — a regular one and another designed specifically for pleasuring one's g-spot. When she checked them out, Autumn discovered they were already loaded with batteries, although the packaging warned these were "not included."

Jessica must have put them in. She smiled, wondering if this was *all* her friend had done with the sex kit.

In the end, of course, it didn't matter, as Autumn stripped naked, climbed into bed, and took care of business. This time, she had the presence of mind to lay down a towel — a decision which proved to be wise as she pleasured herself to three orgasms with her "special" birthday presents.

Nine thirty p.m. Autumn drove home. It had been a decent date. Chaz had taken her to an excellent restaurant for her birthday. Still, she'd been thinking about Jessica the entire time, and when he'd asked if she wanted to catch a movie or do something else, she'd politely declined. The fact was, she'd been eager to get home and wait for Jessica's call.

She arrived at her apartment, shedding her date clothes and donning the Victoria's Secret Pink gear. No sooner had she gotten dressed when the phone rang.

"Oh my God, Jess. Thank you *so much*," Autumn bubbled.

Mock innocence. "For what?"

"My treasure hunt."

"You liked, I hope?"

"Jess, it was *perfect*. All of it." She felt herself getting misty again. "Nobody's ever done anything like that for me. Ever."

"You deserve it. You're wonderful."

Autumn did need to know one thing. "Jess, tell me. Were *you* there today? Did you see me at some point today?"

"Oh, my." The melodious, flirtatious voice again. "Are we playing Truth or Dare already?"

"Nope." Autumn strived to keep it serious. "Truth or truth."

Jessica gave a laugh, but trailed it off. "No. Unfortunately. Like I said, I had to work today. Just got off, in fact."

"But you went to all those stores?" Autumn pressed, still trying to ascertain that her friend was, indeed, local.

"Tell me about your birthday," Jess deflected. "Did you have any trouble following your clues?"

"I think I managed."

"And did you follow them in order?"

Autumn grinned, remembering when she'd tried to "listen ahead" to the second message. "How did you know I'd try to listen before I got to the mall?"

"Because I know you." She chuckled. "Bad girl. Tell me more."

"Well, I went to Starbucks, found my cup."

"I hope you liked it."

"I did, thank you! It took me a few minutes to get the next clue. I'm a ditz sometimes!"

"Did you find—"

"Yes, I eventually figured out Cellular Solutions."

"So, you got the Bluetooth."

"Talking on it right now!"

"Ooooooh. So, both your hands are free. And what are they doing?"

"Nothing..." *Yet.* "The clue about the uniforms took me a *long* time. I had to wander for a while to get that one."

"Uniforms? Oh, yeah. Roleplay."

"Yes. But I found Spencer's. Met Casey."

"Casey." Jessica's soft, reflective tone suggested that she might be acquainted with the young Goth woman outside of her capacity as the clerk at Spencer's Gifts. Again, her belly stirred with a hint of jealousy.

"I got my very interesting presents there. Had to explain privacy laws too," she reminisced with a smile, elaborating about the HIPAA conversation.

"And how did *that* topic come about?" Again, the timbre of Jessica's voice suggested she already knew more than she was letting on, or at least she suspected.

"I don't quite remember," Autumn lied, evading the

topic of how she'd grilled the various mall employees about Jessica.

"I see. So, have you... *tried out* any of those gifts?"

Autumn thought about her "afternoon delight" with the two sex toys. "Well, um," she said, flustered, "it's not like the Truth or Dare is a one-player game."

"Uh huh. And the *other* present?"

"I... uh... it was a great gift! I liked it."

Jess chuckled slowly.

"What?"

"It's just *so* adorable, Autumn. You have this cute little habit of answering my questions by *not* answering them."

"And then," Autumn rushed to change the subject, "the 'time out' hint was *really* clever."

"Ah. The special refreshments."

"Yes, those. You sure know the way to my heart, Jess."

"Really?" Jessica said thoughtfully.

"I meant—"

"Nice subject change, by the way."

"Uh..."

"Have you cracked any of the 'refreshments' open yet?"

"No, of course not." Autumn smiled. "I wanted to wait for you!"

"That's sweet, Autumn. I think I might even have a shot glass around here... *somewhere...*"

Autumn grinned foolishly as she reminisced about the "special" photo Jess had left her.

"Any idea where I might find one?"

She's wondering if I found the photo, Autumn realized, recalling that it had been well-hidden in the bottom of the Things Remembered box.

"I have one here. It says, 'Great minds' on it."

"Aw, I just wish I had one of my own."

"Maybe, try checking, um..." Autumn grinned shyly. "Between your breasts?"

A slow laugh. "Oh, *there* it is! Things tend to get lost between there."

I'd sure love to.

Autumn blinked. "I liked the Victoria's Secret surprises too."

"I hope so. Did they fit okay?"

"Perfect. I'm wearing them right now! And I saw what you wrote on the tag," she needled, a reference to the "*girl*friend pants."

"I bet you look cute in them."

"Nah, I'm just sort of..." She paused, then grinned. "Well, yeah. Kinda." She giggled. "Okay. Yeah, I'm rocking them."

"I'm glad."

"And then, I have this *decadent* looking cinnamon roll."

"Oh, yeah?"

"Why, yes. I believe it's called a *PecanBon*."

Jess paused, seemingly thoughtfully. "Oh. Well, oddly

enough, I just *happen* to have one in front of me too."

"*Mmm*. Does yours have a candle in the middle of it?"

"No," her phone pal intoned with mock sadness. "No candle. But then, I'm not the birthday girl, either."

"Thank you again, Jess. It was really sweet."

"So, light the candle."

She found a match and did so. "Okay, it's lit. Is this like my birthday cake?"

"Exactly."

"Works for me."

"Now hush." And Jess broke into a special rendition of *Happy Birthday*. As it turned out, her smooth, vibrant phone voice also translated into a rather sweet singing voice.

"Thank you," said Autumn again when she'd finished.

"Now you have to make a wish. And don't tell me, or it won't come true."

"Okay."

Autumn thought and wished. *I hope this will be the year I can find happiness.* As she blew out the candle, she couldn't help but wonder if her wish would come true... and, if the person on the phone with her might be involved with it in some way.

"Was it a good one?"

"Very."

"I hope it comes true, Autumn."

She smiled. "Part of it already has."

"Yeah?"

"Yeah. I'm talking to you, aren't I?"

"Oh... how sweet."

"Everything was perfect, Jess. And I loved the shot glasses, too."

"Great minds think alike."

Amused, Autumn noticed that her friend's voice was somewhat muffled—as if she were chewing on a cinnamon roll.

"I almost didn't find the key. Or the... um..."

"Picture?" Jess took a couple of seconds, presumably to finish her bite of *PecanBon*. "Yeah, that's me. Well, some of me."

When do I get to see the rest?

"I liked it. You're beautiful, Jess."

"Thank you. Believe it or not, I'm super shy."

"Nah, I don't believe that."

"I am." Her voice went lower. "I'm just really comfortable with you."

"Well... I'm comfortable with you too."

"You're having an okay birthday?"

"I'm having a *perfect* birthday." She grinned. "I loved the other gifts too. You even remember that I love Olive Garden. And the music globe literally made me cry. Jess, you shouldn't have."

"It was nothing. Really."

"No, it was something. It was everything." Again,

Autumn felt her voice cracking ever so slightly and hoped Jess wouldn't catch it.

She did. "Hey, now. Supposed to be a happy birthday. How about a drink?"

"Fine by me. Hope you have some vodka over there too?"

"Yeah, like I wouldn't make sure *I* was covered too?" Jess chuckled.

They drank and talked some more. They didn't crack open the Truth or Dare game, but as the vodka flowed, the chat got friskier and more amorous.

"Are you still wearing the Pink gear?"

"Yes, I love it. *Very* comfortable. Thanks, Jess."

"You know, there was something else in the box. Which I bet would be even *more* comfortable."

The silky robe of Jessica's. Autumn's cheeks burned at the thought.

"Did you try it on?"

"N-not yet."

"I love how it feels against my bare skin. Try it."

"I was going to wait till—"

"Do it."

Autumn shrugged out of her top, and then peeled off the "girlfriend pants." Hastily, as if Jess were able to see her, she put on the robe and tied it shut.

"Okay."

"How does it feel?"

"You're right, it feels great against, um, against my skin."

"Describe." Jessica's voice was laced with excitement.

"Well... it's... really soft against my skin. Silky..."

"It's almost like being naked. And doesn't leave much to the imagination."

"Nope."

"Is the front open?"

"It's... I have it tied."

"Undo it."

"But... I just put it on."

"Untie it. I want to show you what I did the last time I wore it."

All at once, Autumn's clit was on fire.

"And, ah, what was that, Jess?"

"I said 'show you.' Untie it."

"Okay." She undid the shoelace-style bow she'd tied. "Done."

"That sash would look great around your wrists."

Autumn gave the tiniest of whimpers. "But then I'd be helpless," she protested in a little-girl voice.

Jessica's low, wicked laugh said *oh, but you already are.*

"I love the way my breasts feel through the fabric." Autumn giggled nervously at that. "Try it."

"Okay, Jess. B-both hands?"

"Yes, sweetie."

Her hands moved to her chest, gently fondling her perky breasts through the nearly paper-thin fabric. She groaned as her already-hard nipples were stimulated.

"How does that feel?"

"Feels terrific..."

"Mmm. This is why I wanted you to have your hands free."

"So... this is what you did the last time you wore this?"

Jessica chuckled. "That's not *all* I did. But yes. I'd lie around and play with my boobs all day if I could."

"Well, you have a lot more to work with than I do. But yeah. I would too."

"Play with your boobs all day?" She paused thoughtfully. "Or... play with *mine* all day?"

"Maybe both," Autumn whispered.

"No complaints here."

Boldly, Autumn went on. "Jessica, tell me what else you did. Or, uh, show me."

"Take your right hand. Slide it underneath the seam. On your belly."

Autumn obeyed.

"Keep playing up top with your left hand."

"Still over the robe?" clarified Autumn, breathless.

"For now."

"My other hand..."

"Slide it lower. Slow." The breathing from Jessica's end of the connection was a little heavier as well. "Are you in bed?"

"I have this easy chair." Autumn's hand slid down, passing her tummy, her fingers trailing across her abdomen. "I'm just laid back in it."

"Wish I was there. Crawling across the room toward you."

Autumn moaned. Now, she desperately needed extra attention down there. The thought of Jessica on all fours...

"Wh-what would you... ahh... be wearing..." Her hand descended lower.

"Go slow, Autumn," her friend admonished, as if sensing her eagerness. "Well, seeing as how you're wearing my robe, I suppose I'd be wearing... nothing."

This, in turn, conjured the image of Jessica's large breasts, swinging and bouncing as she drew closer. Coupled with the thought of what she'd do to Autumn when she arrived. *Jess, on her knees, looking up at me...*

"Where's your hand?"

"It's, ah..." In spite of all the naughty talk they'd shared, Autumn *still* felt a bit squeamish at using certain words and terms. "Fingers are, uh, just above..."

"Ah. Good, Autumn." She gave a long, satisfied moan. "This is the part where I slid my left hand underneath the robe, and started playing with my right breast. That means do that too, Autumn," she added in the way of clarification.

"Okay." She slipped her hand into the robe, just as the fingers of her other hand grazed her clit. "Jess, what are you doing over there?"

"Talking to you. And listening to you."

"Maybe you should—"

"Is it my birthday?" A pause. "How about you just lie back... do as you're told... and let this be about you?" It wasn't a request.

Autumn's clit was already swollen and aroused, and she turned her attention to it, rubbing in slow, deliberate circles. Her breathing instantly grew more labored, and she was purring and whimpering with regularity.

"Sounds like you're doing exactly what I did."

"Yeah, I think I am."

"Mmm."

"What did you... do next, Jess?"

A naughty chortle. "Why, I made myself come, of course."

"Sounds like a good plan," Autumn breathed, picking up speed.

"Let me know when you get close."

"*Mmm*, I will."

It didn't take all that long, thanks to everything Jessica had said and done today. Autumn was quivering all over and had never been as turned on in her life.

"I'm... ah... almost..."

"Slide your hand back up."

"But..."

"Stop touching yourself. Take your hand away."

"Jess, please, I'm almost—"

"Now."

Reluctantly, she moved her hand back up to her bare belly, fingers brushing through her navel. "Okay."

"Are you thinking of me in front of you?"

"Yes. God, *yes.*"

"I'd kiss you."

"Ohhhhhhh..."

"Where do you want me to kiss you?"

"On my mouth."

"Where else?"

"Neck…"

"Mmm delicious. I'm a sucker for that. Anywhere else?"

"Uh… breasts."

"Sounds great. Why don't you bring your right hand back up there? Play with them for me, Autumn."

"Please," Autumn groaned.

"Fondle yourself."

"I am."

"Where else do you like to be kissed?" Autumn could tell her friend was enjoying the buildup. She was on fire, needing attention and relief in the worst way.

"I like… on my thigh…"

"I'd spent a *lot* of time kissing you there."

Dreamily, Autumn recalled the first time she'd fantasized about Jess — specifically, how it might feel to have her phone friend's hair tickling her thighs.

"Jess, please, may I—"

"Not yet." Her voice had taken on an authoritative timbre. "This is called 'edging.'"

"Edging?"

"When you bring yourself right to the edge. And then deny."

"Oh. Is this what... you did?"

"No," said Jess matter-of-factly. "But then, *I* wasn't the one who was a bad girl by listening to the voicemails before she was supposed to."

"Jess, it was just that one."

"But I told you it needed to be punished," Jessica admonished. "You didn't follow the instructions. But you're going to follow them now."

"And what if I don't?" pouted Autumn defiantly.

"Then I'll forbid you from touching yourself at all. Nothing. No Autumn time."

"For how long?"

"However long I please."

"And what makes you think I—"

"Because I know you won't."

This entire line of conversation was giving Autumn a deep, dark thrill — in part, because she realized Jess was right. *I would totally obey her.*

She tried a different tack. "Jess. *Please* let me. I need it."

"And why didn't you think about that when you were disobeying your instructions?"

"Maybe I'm just a bad girl," she purred. "Like you said."

Jess chuckled. "'Maybe'?"

"I *am* a bad girl. Sometimes."

"Well, bad girls need to be punished."

"But it's just because I learned it from you," Autumn pointed out. "I'm sorry for listening to the message. I was just... curious."

"Well, we *do* want you to be more *curious*, don't we?" Jessica delivered her patented sexy, throaty laugh again. "Okay. It *is* your birthday. You may touch yourself again."

Autumn didn't need to be told twice. Her fingers were back on her clit almost immediately.

"*Ooooooooh*. My other hand, should I still—"

"Play with your tits."

"Thank you, Jess."

"What's your other hand doing?"

"I'm... rubbing my clit."

"Faster. Are you close?"

Autumn was, indeed, already very close again. She moaned in the affirmative.

"Wish my mouth was on you, Autumn. My tongue where your fingers are."

Jessica's words shot through Autumn, going straight to her pussy. Without warning, her orgasm struck. "Ohhhhhhhhhhh!!! Jessica... *yes*... ohhhhhhh!" As an afterthought, she gasped, "May I... come... *please*?"

Her friend was giggling. "Oh, Autumn. I think we need to work on the 'following instructions' part."

"Yes," Autumn groaned submissively. "Or you just need to work on... me... *ohhhhhhhhh again, Jess...*" Her eyes were clamped shut, imagining Jessica's tongue on her and how wonderful it might feel.

"Fuck, that's so hot, Autumn."

"You should... *too*," Autumn gasped.

That laugh again. "Already well on my way."

"Good." Autumn pulled her hand away, forcing herself to back off a little to pay more attention to Jess. "Your turn."

Jessica's own moaning was rapidly building to a crescendo. "How about, *our* turn?"

"That works too," Autumn agreed, her fingers going back to work. Soon after, both girls were making lovely "music" over the phone connection as they climaxed together.

After catching a breather, Autumn ended up in bed, enjoying herself as Jessica continued to instruct her and joined in. In the throes of her pleasure, the lucky birthday girl also confessed she'd gotten a "head start" in breaking in her new toys. Jess, ever the "teacher," nevertheless instructed Autumn in multiple techniques to ensure that her friend was "doing it right."

The "phone party" lasted until two in the morning as the two girls pleasured themselves and one another repeatedly. Autumn was only chided once by downstairs neighbors pounding on the ceiling — when Jess had mentioned riding her face and "glazing it like a Krispy Kreme donut," she'd lost all inhibition and had treated Jess, and the entire apartment building, to an ear-splitting orgasm. Deliriously, she'd wondered if it was the same woman from the "cup of sugar" escapade.

Another work week in the books. It had been pretty busy thanks to a couple of people being let go — although Autumn herself was safe.

She'd gone on a few more dates with Chaz, although she knew him to be "playing the field" and dating other people. She could hardly say anything. Her own dating profiles and a *craigslist* post were still active — though the latter netted her little more than an inbox full of "dick pics." So, every few days, she'd go on a blind date, more often than not ending up home by ten p.m. to commiserate with Jessica.

Jess was still keeping it mysterious via the *UNKNOWN CALLER* mask — although Autumn now felt 95% certain her phone friend must be local. Thinking back upon the birthday treasure hunt, (a.k.a. *the sweetest thing anyone has ever done for me*), it was highly improbable someone from a distant locale could have, or would have, set up something like that.

Then again... Jess was Jess.

The two would usually swap work stories or discuss Autumn's latest dating crash-and-burn. If Jessica was actively dating, she hadn't made mention of it. And then, as the hour grew later, and the vodka flowed more freely, the talk would sometimes get spicy and racy. It didn't get *quite* as raunchy as it had during the Truth or Dare night — but, on more than one occasion, idle chit-chat gave way to heavy breathing, loud buzzing, and passionate moaning.

Tonight, there was no date, so Autumn had just kicked

her shoes off and was relaxing. She checked her phone, and to her surprise, there was a new voicemail message.

How does she do that without the phone actually ringing?

She played the message. It was short — just three sentences.

"Go to the Four Seasons. There's something for you at the concierge desk. Bye, sweetie."

All at once, Autumn again had that sensation of butterflies in her stomach. *What's there for me? Another gift? It's not even my birthday.*

She played the message back again. As always, Jessica's voice had that special *something* that struck a chord with Autumn. But unlike the birthday surprise messages, there was something else. Something uncharacteristic of Jess. After listening to the brief message for the third time, she identified it as nervousness.

What would she have to be nervous about? Unless...

Forty minutes later, Autumn was rocking her little black dress and stiletto heels, heading downtown.

As her eyes scanned the hotel lobby, carefully

scrutinizing any guest with red hair, Autumn was again reminded of the extremely odd nature of the "relationship" with Jessica. "Red hair and big boobs," she murmured to herself.

Really, Autumn. That's all you know?

How about actually cares about you?

Takes time out to talk and laugh with you?

Makes you feel special? Like you matter?

Those *don't count?*

All at once, Autumn felt like she didn't deserve any of this. And that Jessica — wherever she might be — deserved much better. *A better friend. Or... whatever.*

With a sigh, she willed herself to shut down the pity party and to get a grip. Her friend had sent her here to collect *some* sort of gift, and, if it were anything remotely like the effort she'd put into Autumn's birthday, it would be something very special.

Adjusting herself and turning her frown upside down, she strode purposefully toward the concierge desk.

Are you watching me from somewhere, Jessica? Just in case the answer was *yes*, she took care to swivel her hips ever so slightly. Her ass looked very nice in this particular dress, if Autumn did say so herself, and if it swayed back and forth a bit, so much the better.

As she crossed the room, there were indeed several sets of eyes on her, although no well-endowed redheads. Still, she felt the slightest twinge of excitement at the added attention.

"Good evening, welcome to the Four Seasons, miss."

Autumn smiled back. "Hi. Good evening," she corrected herself. "I'm... supposed to pick something up here?"

"Name, miss?"

"Autumn—" She realized that Jess didn't even know her last name. "Just Autumn."

Ooooooh now that *sounds classy as hell,* she mocked herself.

"Ah, yes, miss. Right here."

As she saw what was in the concierge's hand, her eyes grew wider and her pulse quickened. With a deep breath,

185

trying to collect herself, she took it.

The elevator doors opened, and she stepped out into the empty corridor.

The bronze sign on the wall with an arrow to the left declared 800 — 809. To the right, 810 — 819.

She eyed the black keycard in her hand, turning it over. 817.

Uncertainly, she headed to the right.

The odd-numbered rooms were on the left. *811...* *813...* Her heart began to beat faster as the numbers got larger.

Number 817 had a *Do Not Disturb* tag hanging from the door handle, right beneath the slot which would accept the keycard she was holding. Autumn stood there for a long moment.

Do I knock? Go in?

Is Jess in there?

What if she takes one look at you and tells you to get lost?

What if the room is empty? Like in high school, when they invited you to that "party" and it was just a vacant lot?

How dare you think that of Jessica?

Why am I so nervous?

She raised the keycard, but her trembling hand stopped, an inch away from the slot.

I can't do this.

She swallowed, took a deep breath.

Lowering the keycard, she raised her hand to knock on the door instead.

What if she can't answer? Like, if she's in the shower?

Or tied to the bed waiting for you?

What if she looks through the peephole and doesn't want *to answer?*

Now Autumn was shaking, all the conflicting emotions playing on her at once. Excitement. Insecurity. Joy. Vulnerability. Anticipation. Fear.

She made a fist, prepared to knock.

If she wanted you to knock, why would she have left you a keycard? She lowered her hand, raised the keycard again. It took several seconds to will her hand to remain steady enough to get the keycard into its slot.

She inserted the card, expecting some sort of "response" from the door mechanism. No green light, no little *click*. She pushed the handle down, but the door didn't move.

She left me a phony card, probably to play a mean joke on me.

Right. Or, maybe you didn't do it correctly?

Autumn looked at the card, flipping it over again to find an arrow and a *This Side Up*.

Wow, I'm an idiot.

Well, if she's in the room, she knows I'm here now.

What the fuck am I doing?

Now her trembling was almost uncontrollable. Again, she tried to still her hand enough to insert the card properly. At this point, not even sure she *wanted* to.

I'll just knock.

I should just go.

She's in there. She knows I'm here. She would have opened the door if she wanted to.

She's probably not in there. She probably bought me another gift and needed somewhere to leave it for me to pick it up.

Yeah, right. She's going to buy a four-hundred-dollar hotel room just to leave a present. She would have just left it with the concierge.

I don't know what to do.

She raised her hand again to knock.

Down the hall in the direction she'd come, the elevator chimed its arrival.

Autumn panicked, her fist pausing just as it was about to rap on the hotel door. As the elevator doors slid open, she turned in the opposite direction, hurrying away toward the end of the corridor and the sign marked EXIT. One of her heels caught on the carpet, causing her to stumble. She crouched, kicking off the stilettos and scooping them up, continuing barefoot toward the exit.

From behind her, she heard one of the doors begin to open. Perhaps the very one she'd been standing in front of for the past five minutes.

Stop. Go back.

But she didn't. She hit the door handle at a dead run, pushing it open and escaping into the stairwell, where she took the stairs two at a time all the way down to the lobby. She didn't even stop long enough to put her stilettos back on, nor to catch her breath for that matter, until she finally found herself in the safety of her car.

Coward, she thought as she turned the ignition. Breathless, heart still pounding, she put the car in drive.

Autumn drove aimlessly for a while, then headed for home. Back in her apartment, she ditched the black dress and heels, shrugging into her favorite oversized nightshirt while twisting the cap off the cranberry vodka.

She was there. Why didn't I...?

She drank, picking up her phone and looking through it as she did so. No new calls, so she set the phone back on the end table, ready to snatch it up if it rang — and, at the same time, knowing she wouldn't be able to bring herself to actually answer if Jess called.

What the fuck is wrong with me?

She had the Four Seasons keycard between her fingers, toying with it and flipping it over and over.

I could have just gone into the room, I was right there.

"Jessica, I'm sorry..."

She checked the smartphone again. No calls.

Eventually, she drifted into an uneasy sleep in her easy chair.

PART THREE

AUTUMN & JESS

Midmorning. The sun was already well into the sky when Autumn sat up blearily. Immediately, she checked her phone. No missed calls. No messages.

Coffee.

She popped a pod in the Keurig, placing her Starbucks "heart" tumbler, the gift from Jess, beneath the handle. While it brewed, she checked the phone again, just in case she'd somehow missed any messages or calls. Nothing.

Once she'd sipped some of her coffee, she began to feel a bit more awake. In her mind, she replayed the previous evening, culminated by her mini-meltdown and subsequent flight from the Four Seasons.

Please call me, Jessica.

I should have just opened the door.

What if she never talks to me again?

She will.

I *wouldn't if someone did that to* me.

Autumn wished she had *some* way to get in touch. The mysterious nature of the private calls had been a source of excitement and intrigue, but now...

Maybe she's still at the hotel.

"What the fuck am I doing?" she asked the empty apartment.

Quickly, she grabbed a shower, then got dressed. Today, it was the crop-top Pink Nation shirt and the VS "girlfriend" pants.

Some "girlfriend" you are, Autumn.

Ten minutes later, she was in the car, heading back downtown.

The 8th floor looked different today — less overwhelming. As she exited the elevator, Autumn was nervous for different reasons this time.

What if I've fucked it up? Whatever "it" is?

What if I meet her and she just walks right past me and doesn't say a word? Because that's what I deserve.

Will she still be there? Will the keycard still work?

As she approached 817, she saw she wouldn't need it. The door was slightly ajar, with the latch engaged to keep it from closing all the way. The *Do Not Disturb* hanger was gone.

Taking a deep breath, she pushed the door open. "Jessica?"

The room was empty. She peered into the bathroom anyway, calling her friend's name a few more times. There were used towels on the floor. The king-sized bed had not been slept in, but near the window was a large easy chair with a table next to it. On the table were a couple of miniature vodka bottles — pineapple and mango flavored. They were of the same brand as the miniatures Autumn had gotten for her birthday. Both were empty. Around the neck of one of the bottles, part of a fire-engine red lip print. In the chair were a blanket and a pillow, as if the room's occupant had spent the night in the easy chair.

She was here. For me. And I ran.

She looked out the window. It overlooked the city, lazy and quiet on a Saturday morning. But in her mind's eye, she could imagine how it would have looked last night, everything lit up and beautiful. And, how this room would have looked in soft light, rather than in broad daylight as it was now.

I could have been in that bed with Jess. The thought made her feel nervous, excited, scared, and empty all at the same time. *Or we could have just talked. Or gone out. Spent time together.*

It's not my fault. I told her I was straight.

That's a weak cop out, and you fucking well know it. Besides, how "straight" were you, the other night when you were both—

"Hello?" The voice from behind her nearly made her jump a foot in the air.

She spun around, startled, hoping — and fearing — that Jessica had returned. But it was just one of the housekeeping staff. According to the Four Seasons name tag, this was *MAGDALENA*.

"Housekeeping," the middle-aged woman announced in slightly broken English. "I'm sorry, did not know you were still here."

"No," said Autumn hastily, "I'm not the—" She hesitated. "Yes. I was just leaving. I'll just be a few minutes?"

Magdalena nodded, pushing her cleaning cart back

into the hallway. "Is okay. I come back."

Autumn sat down in the plush easy chair. *She slept here. After I bailed on her.* She reclined against the pillow. The clean linen smell was interlaced with the scent of freshly washed hair. And, on the blanket, the slightest trace of perfume. The same scent as the pink robe Jess had given her for her birthday.

She lingered there for a long while, eyes studying the room. It was beautiful, extravagant. *A great place to spend time with someone special. Or not.*

She looked toward the door.

I was on the other side of that door. I should have just come in. She frowned as she wondered how Jessica must have felt. Certainly, she'd heard Autumn fumbling with the door, and then nothing. Just ditched with no explanation whatsoever.

"I'm sorry, Jess," she whispered, a tear sliding down her cheek. She sat there for a long while, until she heard Magdalena's cart bustling around in the corridor again. Autumn stood, collecting herself. On her way out, she took the lip-printed vodka bottle, tucking it into her purse.

The rest of Saturday was what Autumn thought of as a "self-pity" day, which meant malingering around the apartment, sipping vodka and getting nothing done. And receiving no phone calls from *UNKNOWN* numbers. She talked with Stephanie, who stopped by an hour or so after Autumn got back.

"I brought Chinese," her friend announced, holding up the familiar white cartons.

"Thanks."

"So, what's going on?"

Autumn didn't really feel like talking about it and politely said as much. Steph assumed it was a blind date gone bad, as usual, and Autumn didn't correct her.

Her friend tried to get her off the couch, suggesting a night out, but Autumn declined. "Go without me; have fun. We'll get together soon."

Sunday was more of the same, except she did venture out of the apartment when Chaz invited her to "hang out." This lasted about an hour and a half, with Autumn constantly checking her phone.

"I'm not very good company today," she'd finally explained. "I'm just going to go home. I'll call you." The rest of the evening, more vegging on the couch, Netflix, and vodka. And no calls from Jess.

What did you expect, Autumn?

Monday, she dragged herself to work, still in a funk. She kept her phone with her, even during the weekly marketing meeting, ready to duck out if the *UNKNOWN CALLER* alert showed up. Nothing, other than a message from Chaz making sure she was doing okay.

That one is one of the good ones. One of the few left out there.

Nine p.m. She was finishing dinner, leftover Chinese, when her smartphone buzzed. *UNKNOWN CALLER.* She practically dove across the counter for it.

"Jess!"

"Hi." A deep breath. "Autumn... I'm—"

"Jess," she blurted, "I'm *so* sorry. I just... totally freaked out, like just for a minute, and I wish so bad I could go back. Fuck, I know I let you down, I'm sorry."

A pause. "Are you through?" Jessica asked dryly — although with a hint of amusement?

"Uh... yeah?"

"Don't interrupt when someone is apologizing."

"Huh?"

"Four Seasons. I put you on the spot. I shouldn't have done it that way."

"Jess—"

"Sometimes I can be a little too impulsive, and I *really* want to meet you. And I pushed too hard."

She said "want" and not "wanted." Present tense is good. The thought lifted some of the despair and worry she'd felt over the past three days.

"I should have taken you into consideration a little more. *I'm* sorry."

Cautiously, Autumn spoke. "I... miss you."

"I miss you, too."

"Jess... I wish I had—"

"I know." The soft, hypnotizing voice, soothing her again. "We have plenty of time."

"Are you okay?"

"Yes. And *we're* okay, Autumn," Jessica reassured. "But I *do* have to work really early. So, I'll call you?"

"Yes."

"Good night, Autumn. Sweet dreams."

Things went pretty much back to "normal" over the next several days. Jessica would call in the morning or the later evening, and they'd chat, discuss whatever dating misadventures Autumn might be having, or whatever else was going on in their lives. Some of the conversations continued to get rather steamy and explicit. Once, Jess even called Autumn during her lunch hour, making her friend retreat to her car with explicit instructions to pleasure herself. Another time, it was an impromptu "movie night," with both girls hanging out on the phone while watching a steamy movie together.

Jessica said nothing more about the Four Seasons, and

Autumn didn't bring it up either. As far as she knew, Jess was unaware she'd gone back the following morning and visited the room. Certainly, her friend's feelings must have been hurt by the entire episode, although she'd downplayed it when they'd initially talked about it.

Although things stayed lighthearted, Jess didn't push for them to go further, other than continuing to stimulate and test Autumn's boundaries during their rather steamy phone escapades, and Autumn didn't try to pry or snoop for more details about her friend.

That is, until Jessica's birthday, when everything changed.

"Good morning, gorgeous."

"Hi. Happy birthday, Jess."

"Thank you."

"Doing anything fun today?"

"Working," Jessica sighed. "As usual."

Autumn gasped. "On your *birthday*? That's awful!"

"Tell me about it. Yeah, gotta work till seven." A pause. "Are you around tonight?"

"I have a date. Supposed to go to a party."

"Oh." Jess sounded disappointed.

"Call me. I'll bail early."

"No, you shouldn't do that—"

"It's okay."

"Autumn," Jessica said slowly, "if I'm getting in the way of anything—"

"No! Goodness, no, Jess. My friend Steph set me up for a blind date. A few weeks ago. 'A friend of a friend' type of thing. I'm more or less humoring her." She paused. "Seriously. Call me when you get off."

"You sure?"

"Absolutely. I love talking to you."

"I love talking to you too."

"Happy birthday, Jessica."

"Thanks, sweetie. Bye."

Autumn sipped her glass of wine, mingling with other party guests. As it turned out, her "date" had brought her to a party his ex-girlfriend was attending — probably on purpose — and he'd steadfastly ignored Autumn for the past forty minutes while chatting with her. *Thanks, Steph.*

"You okay?" A woman about Autumn's age was looking at her intently. Brian had introduced her earlier — this was Brenda, a coworker of his who was also hosting the party.

"Yeah, fine." Autumn offered up a smile. "It's a nice party."

"Meh." Brenda took a drink of her beer. "I don't even know most of these people. Brian's about the only one I know outside of my department." She shrugged. "Oh well, they brought food. So, there's that."

Autumn laughed at that. "Yeah. Food's always good."

"Well, help yourself." Brenda looked toward the next room, where Autumn's "date" and his ex were on the couch, intently engaged in conversation. She grimaced.

"Sorry about…"

"No worries. Pretty much a blind date; a friend trying to fix me up."

"Ah, one of those."

Autumn killed her wine, glancing toward the closed door off the kitchen. "Is someone in the bathroom, do you know?"

"Yeah, someone just went in there. There's one upstairs though. Here, I'll show you the way."

They went upstairs. Autumn headed for the first door in the hallway.

"Not that one. That's my sister's room. She's in Europe."

"Nice."

Brenda pointed. "Down the hall, second to last on the right."

"Thanks."

Autumn freshened up and checked herself in the mirror. *All in all*, she reflected, *I've got it going on.* She hadn't accepted tonight's date with the thought of landing a husband, but Brian could at least show *some* interest?

I'll bet Jessica would if she were here.

She bit her lip, giggling at the thought, and hoped her friend was having a nice birthday—wherever she was. *She ought to be off work by now... hopefully.* And, hopefully, Autumn would get a call tonight.

Maybe she wants to go out and enjoy herself instead of hanging out at home alone, drinking vodka in PJs and talking on the phone... like some *people.*

Back downstairs, her date was now nowhere to be found. Autumn did her best to mingle — it wasn't exactly her strong suit — but the most interesting thing she found was the taco salad dip. It went *great* with Doritos, so she had a couple helpings of it.

"Enjoying the dip?" Another of the party guests, who looked to be a later thirty-something, was grabbing refills on beer. "I made that."

"Yes. It's delicious! You did a great job. Do you have the recipe for that?"

"I got it off allrecipes dot com. Just search *taco salad dip,* and it's like the first one listed."

"Thanks. I'll have to try it!"

Brenda breezed back into the kitchen. "Hey there. Autumn, right? You getting enough to eat?"

Autumn nodded. "I'd say so."

"Dig in. There's plenty, and I have to either send it home with someone or make room in the fridge."

"Thanks. It's great. But I might be taking off before long."

Brenda frowned. "Aww. So soon? The night's young!"

"Yeah." She looked around. "Any idea where my *date* is?"

"Not too sure." She turned to the older woman. "Lisa, have you seen Brian around?"

"I think he might be upstairs," Lisa mused.

"Cool. Thanks." Autumn put her empty plate in the trash and headed that way.

The upstairs bathroom was empty. On a hunch, she checked the main bedroom, which had a master bath. Nobody there either.

He better not have left with that floozy. True, she hadn't been "feeling" this date since it started, but Autumn deserved some basic courtesy. She shrugged and headed back to the stairs. As she passed the first bedroom — the one belonging to the "sister in Europe" — she noticed the door was slightly ajar. She opened it.

"Brian?" She peered into the room. "Hello?" A small reading lamp was on at the desk, but nobody was there. She turned to leave.

A noise from within the room stopped her.

"Hello?"

Curious, she stepped into the bedroom. The noise was coming from the closet, and by the time she'd made it halfway across the room, she'd pretty much figured out what it was. She grabbed the knob and threw the door open anyway.

Her date and his ex-girlfriend were locked in an embrace, standing in the center of the walk-in closet. His tongue was halfway down her throat, and several of the buttons on her blouse were already undone.

"Are you *fucking* kidding me?" Autumn said softly.

The woman broke the kiss. "*Heyyyyy.* It's a *party* now," she murmured, slurring her words slightly. Brian looked somewhat surprised, guiltily removing his hand from her partially exposed, milky-white breast.

"Uh... hey, Amber..." He grinned weakly at her.

"*Autumn!*" she corrected him ferociously.

"Autumn," he amended, "I, we, uh..."

"*Get out!*" Her eyes blazed at them. "Get the *fuck* out of here!" Although it wasn't her house, nor her closet, they both quickly scrambled for the door.

She sank down to a sitting position, cross-legged. A few tears had begun to flow. No, she hadn't been "into" Brian in the first place, and had just met him, *but am I ever gonna find a decent guy?*

"What the fuck is *wrong* with me?" she asked the empty closet, now sniffling.

Just then, her phone rang.

Without checking it, she answered: "*What?*"

"Whoa," came Jessica's soft voice. "Are you okay?"

"Just... *peachy,*" Autumn sneered. She began telling Jess about her latest in the endless line of dating failures, but stopped herself.

It's her birthday. Why spoil it with my pity party?

"Happy birthday, Jess. Are you having a good day?"

"I was, but now I'm worried about *you!*" The voice was full of concern. "What's bothering you?"

"Just... the usual." She sniffled again.

"The usual? Isn't that vodka for you? Or flashing your boobs for your apartment complex?"

Damn you, Jessica! You make it impossible *for a girl to wallow in self-pity!* She pursed her lips, pausing for a couple of seconds.

You know what? Fuck it. She grabbed the sleeve of one of Sister-in-Europe's cardigans, wiping one last stubborn tear away.

"Jess. Where are you right now?"

"Just got home a little while ago. Now making a run to the store."

Autumn thought for a second. "By any chance... is the store anywhere near Arbor Hills?"

"Yes," said Jess thoughtfully. "Yes, I think it is."

Going through her smartphone, Autumn pulled up the GPS app which was still open in the background.

Fuck it, she told herself again.

"Forget the store. Go to..." She chose the last destination entry. "4231 Simkins Court."

"And what will I find there?" Her voice dropped to a suggestive whisper. "Are *you* there?"

"Just *go there*," Autumn ordered. "Now." *Before I change my mind.*

"You know, you're kind of bossy, miss," Jessica criticized, very stern and reproachful. But then, slowly, she began to chuckle. "I like it. I like it a *lot.*"

From the background, she could hear an artificially

intelligent voice: *Starting Route To 4231 Simkins Court. Arbor Hills.* And then: *Call ended.*

What the fuck did I do?

As she waited, Autumn nervously primped herself in Sister-in-Europe's armoire mirror. With a glance toward the closed door, she opened the top drawer in the armoire, then the next one down. She kept looking till she found what she'd hoped: a pair of black silk scarves. She partially folded one up and laid it on the bed, doing the same with the second one before retreating back to the walk-in closet with it.

The phone announced her UNKNOWN CALLER again. Heart racing, she answered it.

"I'm here. Now what?" Laughter. "Oooooh, looks like there's a party. Can I come?"

Now Autumn was drawing deep breaths, willing herself not to hyperventilate.

"Come—" She stopped. Her voice was coming out all wobbly. She cleared her throat. "Come in the front door.

Go past the kitchen to—"

"I just walk in? Won't someone say something?"

"No. She doesn't even know half the people here. If anyone asks, say you work in..." *What department did my asshole date say?* "Accounts Payable. Go to the stairs—"

"So, you *are* here." Jessica's voice reflected excitement, thinly masked with amusement. "If I didn't know better, I'd be thinking someone likes m—"

"Jess. My heart is fucking *pounding*," Autumn whispered.

"Mine too, sweetie."

Thirty seconds later, the Bluetooth relayed the sound of a couple of people talking, one maybe somewhat drunk. One of them apparently greeted Jess.

"Hey, how's it going?" Jessica, nonchalantly acting as if she belonged there, continued on. Her voice was hushed. "I'm at the front door."

"Go in," croaked Autumn.

"Are you sure?"

No! And please don't ask me that!

"Jess. Wh-what if you don't like me?"

"Not a possibility, Autumn."

She exhaled. "Go in."

A few moments later, the sound of the front door closing — both via the phone connection and within actual earshot.

Now Autumn was shaking so badly she almost dropped the phone.

She's in the house.

To the best of Autumn's knowledge, the two of them had only been this close one other time — at the Four Seasons. Before she'd panicked and—

That's not *going to happen now.*

"Now what?"

A few tears began to flow now. These were the good kind, Autumn reflected — *much* better than the ones she'd wasted earlier on Brian and others like him.

"On the other side of the kitchen. The stairs..."

More voices over the phone. Autumn recognized Brenda's. "How are you doing?"

Fuck. Busted. Now, Jessica would be asked to leave. Part of Autumn — the part that wanted to run and hide and never take any chances — felt slightly relieved.

But Jessica spoke up without missing a beat. "Oh, you know how Accounts Payable is. Slave drivers..."

"I feel ya." Momentary silence as Brenda bought it. "Well, there's plenty of food. Whatever doesn't go, I have to find a place for... so eat up."

"Thanks. I *am* very hungry."

A moment later, Brenda could be heard talking to a couple of other guests — and, growing fainter. And now, the sound of Jessica on the stairs. Autumn could hear the footfalls from outside the room now.

Jessica's sweet whisper, "Okay. Where am I going?"

Home. Turn around and go home. I'm sorry, Jess, I'm going to chicken out. Again. But there was only one way out — the stairs.

Quit being such a baby. You are not *going to fuck this up like the Four Seasons.*

"Autumn, are you still there?"

A deep breath. "First room on the, uh, left."

Now she heard the footsteps outside the door. The door handle turning. Opening.

She's in the room now.

"Okay. I'm here..."

"Lock the door," Autumn whispered, her voice trembling.

She heard the door shut and the click of the push-button lock.

"There's... something on the bed for you."

"Mmm. Wish it were you," Jess teased, although she now sounded as nervous as Autumn felt. "Let's see. Hmm. Blindfold?"

She could hear her friend's voice, even without the phone, she was that close. *She's less than ten feet away.* Autumn's hands were shaking so badly, she was struggling to hold the phone.

"Yes. Put it on, and…"

"And?"

Fuck…

In the dark closet, behind her own blindfold, the sound of her heart racing madly drowned out all else. Except for Jessica's sweet voice.

"Autumn?"

She exhaled. "Put the blindfold on, and… open the closet."

Autumn didn't toss the phone down so much as lose her grip on it thanks to her trembling hands. Either way, it bounced softly on the carpet.

Get a grip… relax…

But then the door opened. Autumn whimpered, almost inaudibly.

"Autumn?" Her friend's familiar voice — in person for the first time.

"Jess. Happy birthday."

"Th-thank you."

In the darkness, she stepped toward the wonderful sound. And then... hands on her shoulders.

"Oh..." Jessica's whisper. She, too, was trembling. Autumn's arms wrapped around her friend, embracing her. A second later, she felt Jessica's lips on the corner of her mouth, planting a kiss but missing the mark somewhat. She turned her head slightly, and their lips made a more solid connection for the second kiss... the third. By the fourth, her mouth was open slightly, and Jess wrapped both her lips around Autumn's lower one, sucking it and giving it a love-nibble.

"*Mmm*..." Her fingers ran through Jessica's hair. *Red,* she thought, although of course she couldn't see it. She felt the line of the silk scarf/makeshift blindfold Jess was wearing and eased away from it lest she accidentally pull it loose. Not that it would matter much in the lightless closet.

"Jess."

Her friend's tongue slid into her mouth this time, and Autumn welcomed it, met it with her own. She'd never kissed another woman, and this was entirely different than kissing a guy. Different... and better. They continued the passionate kiss for a few minutes. Autumn's hands explored Jessica's face, her shoulders, her hips. Jess was a little bolder, squeezing Autumn's ass and then running her hands up and down, even getting a couple gropes of "side boob" by the end.

"Oh, Autumn..." Another kiss. When this one tapered off, Jessica laughed. "So, what's this? *Seven Minutes in Heaven?*"

Wistfully, Autumn remembered her friend's *Seven Minutes* anecdote, from their immortal Truth or Dare game. "I don't know. Gonna run from the closet screaming?"

"Maybe *you'll* be the one screaming." Jess laughed softly and moved in for another kiss, this one much more urgent and passionate. And now, her hands tentatively caressed Autumn's breasts through the dress.

"This okay?" whispered Jessica huskily.

"It's *your* birthday." Autumn shrugged. "Open your present." Then they were kissing again — this time with

Autumn as the aggressor. Jessica was working with the top of her dress, peeling it away. And by the time Autumn drew back from the kiss, her breasts were exposed with Jess expertly kneading them.

Both girls mutually sank to a sitting position on the carpet, facing one another, hands wandering while the two explored kiss after kiss. So far, Autumn hadn't quite dared to do the "second base" thing, although her hands flirted with it several times.

"Here," Jessica finally sighed, grabbing Autumn's hands and planting them squarely on her breasts. "I know this is what you want." Then back to kissing. Autumn eagerly caressed her friend's boobs through what felt like a silky blouse. Indeed, her hands discovered a column of buttons in the center, two of which already seemed to be undone. Her fingers and thumbs cautiously approached the third button.

"Mmm-*hmm*," Jess encouraged her. Her own hands soon moved that way to help out — Autumn's fingers were still shaking unsteadily although all of the hot kissing had certainly taken the edge off. There were four more buttons in all, and they got them undone in short order. The blouse fell open, and Autumn's hands now encountered Jessica's bra. It didn't feel lacy, as she'd pictured Jess wearing. But then, she reminded herself, her friend had just barely gotten off work. Her thumbs felt the rigid outline of underwire at the bottom of the bra. Jess was certainly well-endowed.

Autumn's hands snaked around, following the bra toward Jessica's back and encountering the row of clasps there.

Jess gave her a "green light" with another "*Mmm-hmm,*" and soon the bra was out of the way. Autumn trailed her fingertips across her friend's now-bared chest and was rewarded with a quiver, accompanied with a moan of approval. Meanwhile, Jess followed suit, playing with Autumn's smaller breasts in similar fashion.

"Sorry," Autumn murmured between kisses, "afraid I don't have as much."

"What you have is perfect," Jess said reproachfully. Her lips moved down, planting a small trail of kisses till she arrived at Autumn's neck, which she began sucking and nibbling. An electric jolt went straight between her legs, and she threw her head back to bare her neck.

"*Jess...*"

She kissed her way down, continuing the trail and arriving at Autumn's nipples, which she immediately began lashing and teasing with her tongue. They quickly grew hard, prompting Jess to graduate to nibbling. Autumn squirmed, now practically on fire between her thighs. The hypothetical "fire," however, was thankfully balanced out by the cool air hitting her already damp panties.

If she puts her hand down there, she'll find...

Autumn laughed at herself. *That's sorta the idea, isn't it?*

Jessica broke away for a second. "What's funny?"

"Nothing," Autumn assured. "Just... can't believe... you know."

"I know." Back up for a nibble on Autumn's lower lip. "Me neither. You okay?"

"Don't stop. *Please* don't stop."

"*Mmm-mmm.*" Jess shook her head, then went in for another kiss, all the while caressing and fondling. Although Autumn had been somewhat aggressive, she could feel the tide shifting, and her more experienced friend gradually beginning to reassert herself. Jessica's hands trailed their way down to Autumn's outer thighs, and then, the right hand boldly moved over to her right inner thigh. Very tentatively, it slid up, pausing when it encountered the hem of Autumn's dress.

"Is this okay?" Jess asked softly.

"Why not?" Autumn whispered. "It's—" The word *yours* hung on her lips. "It's *your* birthday."

"*Mmm*. Well, I must say I'm *totally* enjoying my present."

"I'm glad," purred Autumn, seeking her friend's lips in the dark for another long kiss. That hand on her thigh kept sliding upward, slowly and deliberately, until it brushed against Autumn's panties.

Her now rather *wet* panties.

Jessica chuckled — a low, sexy laugh that said *I've got you right where I want you*. She didn't waste time, either. Her fingers purposefully slid under the cotton material.

She's going to touch me. And of course, Jess did. Her fingers slipping over Autumn's swollen lips, quickly finding the source of the wetness and pressing forward.

Blushing all over, Autumn was grateful for the darkness and the blindfolds. "I'm... a little excited." She grinned with embarrassment.

"A *little*, huh?" That low, confident right-where-I-want-you chuckle again. Jess slipped her hand farther into her friend's panties, her knuckles pushing the material to the side for better access. She slid two of her fingers in, and right away it was plain that Jessica knew exactly what she was doing, where she was going. This would not be like one of her *craigslist* dates, awkwardly fingering her in some crude attempt to satisfy her before a blowjob.

Jess hooked her fingers, finding Autumn's spot in less than a second.

"*Ohhhhhhhhh.*" She came hard all over Jessica's hand, and then some.

Sister-in-Europe is going to find a strange stain in her closet, she thought detachedly. Then she came a second time, even harder. "*Ooooooooooooh!!!*" She got a little louder, until Jessica's mouth clamped over hers, muffling her pleasure so other party guests wouldn't be alerted to the raunchy activities going on upstairs.

Jessica's other hand came around, those fingers coming in from above and zeroing in on her excited clit. Again, with expert precision, Autumn's special friend knew exactly what buttons to push — and *how* to push them. Autumn began to fall backward from her sitting position, throwing her arms out behind her just in time. If she were to end up lying down, she knew it would be all over — in the sense of Jessica having her way with Autumn.

Yeah, like that would be bad?

"*Jess.*"

"Baby," her phone friend whispered back.

It's her birthday. Shouldn't I be doing something for her?

"Jess... tell me..." She gasped. "What can I... *do.*"

"Come," the sexy voice in the dark ordered. The finger rubbing her clit picked up speed, while the fingers inside her pressed against the throbbing roof of her pussy and held pressure, just where they were needed. And a moment later, she began trembling, quaking from deep within her belly, quickly boiling over into the most explosive orgasm she'd ever had. Deliriously, she put her wrist in her mouth and bit it just to keep her yelps and screams from being heard throughout the house.

Jessica's fingers backed off just enough to keep Autumn on the edge of that wonderful threshold. Every few seconds, an aftershock would rock her womb, causing a fresh volley of moans, and worsening the mess on Sister-in-Europe's carpet. Jess didn't push, seemingly well-aware of how ultra-sensitive Autumn now was. And why *wouldn't* she be? She would certainly know what she herself liked and be able to translate that into Autumn's pleasure, would she not? *If it were a guy, he would be done by now, patting himself on the back and probably grabbing my head for a blowjob.* But Jess certainly wasn't done. Once Autumn's breathing settled down and her trembling abated, she went right back to work, and all at once Autumn was screaming with unadulterated bliss again. This time, she didn't have to muffle her cries with her hand. Jessica had leaned in and was using her tongue for that.

Autumn poured everything into the kiss as Jess rocked her down below. Once more, her talented lover slowed down, keeping the explosive bliss just over the horizon as the aftershocks pleasured her. Waiting just long enough, then going back to it full-throttle, driving Autumn crazy all over again.

After several orgasms, and an indeterminate amount of time (*seconds? hours?*), Autumn could take no more and had to gently paw at Jessica's hands, pushing them away. Jess took the cue, backing off and waiting till her friend had "returned to Earth". And then they were kissing again. Slowly this time, with more sucking than tongue, but absolutely smoldering with passion.

Don't stop, ever.

And they didn't for a long time.

Finally, the kiss did end. As they tapered off, Autumn planted one final smack on Jessica's lips.

"Jessica. *Fuck.*"

Jess laughed. "I feel you. *Mmmmmm.* Happy birthday to *me.*"

That brought a touch of guilt. "Jess, I didn't really do anyth—"

Another full kiss on the lips. Autumn could feel Jessica's smile. "You're *perfect*, Autumn. I couldn't have asked for a better birthday."

"Now what?" Autumn croaked.

"I have to go." She gave Autumn one last explosive kiss, then stood. "I'll call you."

"Jess..."

But she was already leaving. As the closet door opened, though, Autumn did pull the blindfold up to take a peek. As her eyes adjusted, she caught the vague silhouette of her mysterious friend. Jessica was a little shorter than Autumn had imagined her, and perhaps just a touch curvier.

Without looking back, Jess removed her blindfold and tossed it back onto the bed, then strode out of the room and was gone.

It was quite a while before Autumn found the strength to move, let alone get shakily to her knees. Once she managed that, she stood, still wobbly and still basking in the afterglow of the satisfaction she'd just enjoyed. She adjusted her clothing, then emerged warily from the closet (*I'm out of the closet! Get it?* she ribbed herself). Collecting Jessica's blindfold, she laid it out on the bed, smoothed it and folded it neatly, then followed suit with her own scarf. This done, she tucked both scarves back into the drawer where she'd found them and let herself out of the room.

There were no thoughts of *I wonder if she's still here?* Autumn knew Jessica had already left. Cautiously, she descended the stairs, taking care to grip the bannister in case she should swoon.

Navigating the kitchen, she almost ran smack into Brenda.

"Hey, Autumn. I didn't know you were still here." She looked at her guest uncomfortably. "Brian... uh, left." *With his ex-floozy*, she didn't say aloud, although her awkward, apologetic grimace spelled it out.

"I know," Autumn replied quietly.

A frown. "He's a dick. I'm sorry you had such a rotten night, Autumn."

"Yeah. It's been... quite an evening," Autumn replied, straight-faced, even forcing a frown and earning herself a hug from the hostess. "Thanks."

"You're welcome back anytime," Brenda went on. *"He*

won't be. Sorry." She brightened. "Hey, you know what? Why don't you take some food home? I've got some Tupperware containers..."

"Is there any more of the taco dip?"

"*Tons.* Here, grab that container." Brenda grabbed a spoon. "Lisa's gonna be thrilled. This stuff is *great.*"

"Thanks." She hugged Brenda again, then gathered up her leftovers and took her leave of the party.

Autumn lounged in her bed, watching TV, munching on taco salad dip... and trying to wrap her head around what she'd done earlier.

What possessed me?

Why, Jessica did, of course.

Damn. The way she kissed me.

Did I use her to get past my bad date?

Damn. The way I kissed her.

Her fingers. Oh my God.

Is she going to get the wrong idea now?

What makes it the wrong *idea?*

Her racing thoughts were interrupted by the phone. *UNKNOWN CALLER.* Feeling a little awkward about everything, Autumn considered allowing it to just go to voicemail.

Grow up.

"Hello?"

"I can still taste you on my fingers."

A fresh quiver. "Hi there."

"I should have put my tongue on you. You're yummy, Autumn."

"Thanks. I should have... um, done more."

"You did great. And thanks for inviting me."

"Did you have a good birthday?"

"Wonderful. But it's not my birthday anymore." It was true. The alarm clock on the nightstand showed 12:21 a.m.

"Jess?"

"Yeah."

"Was I... you know, okay?"

A sweet laugh. "You're *more* than okay, Autumn. You're amazing."

"Thanks." She hesitated. "So. What do we, um, do now?"

"Mmm." Over the connection, Autumn heard the unmistakable sound of food, probably potato chips, being chomped. "Sorry." Jessica quickly finished off her mouthful of whatever it was she was eating. "Mmm. Hey, did you have time to check out this taco salad dip? That woman at the party... she had tons of it and made me take it home. Mmm, it's *delish*."

More rustling. Not potato chips, but nachos, Autumn realized.

"Um..." Guiltily, she eyed the sizable Tupperware container next to her on the bed, next to the half-eaten bag of Cool Ranch Doritos. "I *think* I might have tried some of it."

"You need to try it. It's great! Damn, I wish I had the

recipe."

"Good night, Jess." Autumn giggled.

"Sweet dreams. About me."

"Oh, I'm sure they will be." Smiling, she ended the call.

Autumn excitedly clawed for her phone on the nightstand and found herself a tad disappointed it wasn't Jess.

"Morning, Steph," she murmured, wiping the sleep from her eyes.

"So. Give me the deets!"

"On what?"

"Your big date, of course! How was Brian?"

"Oh. You'd have to ask his ex."

"Huh? What does that mean?"

As she stumbled to the kitchen for her coffee fix,

Autumn relayed the tale of the party, up to the part where she threw her date and his skank out of the closet.

"Damn, what a bastard. I am *so* sorry, Autumn."

Autumn grabbed her ceramic Starbucks cup from the Keurig tray. "It's not a big deal." She took a sip of her dark roast. "Live and learn."

"You don't sound all that upset."

"Nah. Wasn't really into him anyway."

Stephanie gave a little gasp of surprise. "You're *seeing* someone," she said incredulously.

"No," Autumn said truthfully, "I'm not!"

"You *are*. And... you *got some* last night!"

Autumn was silent on that count.

"Can't fool me. You're *way* too energetic before your coffee."

"I've *got* my coffee!" She held up her "Jess" cup, as if Steph could somehow see it.

"Mmm-hmm. There's someone. Is there someone?"

Not wanting to confess to anything *per se*, Autumn took another swig of coffee.

"Well, *good* for you. Who is it?"

That girl who called me from the blocked number, that you thought might be a crazed stalker? Yeah, she fucked me last night, Steph.

"It's that guy you were with at that thing. The one I met? Charles?"

"You mean Chaz?"

"Yeah, that one. Uh-huh. He was *cute*." Steph gave an approving *hmm*. "Well, you go, girl!"

Autumn remained silent, choosing merely not to answer. *That's not lying, is it?*

"So. Does this mean I don't need to worry about fixing you up anymore? Because I *do* know someone—"

"No, no," Autumn replied hastily. "I think I'll be okay. *More* than okay." With a smile, she recalled Jessica's words. "Actually... amazing."

"Well... okay! Good for you!"

"Lunch soon?"

"You know it! Bye!"

"Hey, beautiful."

"You must have some kind of sixth sense. I *just* slipped into a nice hot bath."

"Oooooooh! Sounds steamy. Have fun. I can call you later."

"*No*," Autumn uttered, a little too emphatically. "I can talk."

"You sure?"

"Yeah."

"Bubble bath?"

"Yep. The one you got me, actually."

"Secret Garden Secret Crush."

"Yes, that."

Jessica sighed. "Long day here. I think there needs to

be a bubble bath in *my* near future too."

"Well, come on in," murmured Autumn, biting her lip shyly as she said it. "There's room for you."

"Oh! You must have one of those luxury tubs."

"Nope, I wish. Just a plain ole standard apartment bathtub. But," she added provocatively, "there's room for you."

"Mmmmmmm. Won't it be crowded?"

"The word you're looking for is *cozy*."

"Nice. Hmmmm, I *do* love the image of a wet, slippery Autumn." She considered for a moment. "I think I *will* join you."

Autumn was almost ready to blurt out her address until she heard the sound of running water in the background. Jessica was referring to "joining her" in the virtual sense, she realized sheepishly.

And, who says she's ready for that *step? Are you, for that matter?* The *Seven Minutes in Heaven* escapade had been a big step (as well as having been positively mind-blowing), but still...

"Still" what?

"What are you up to over there?"

"I'm starting myself a bath, silly. Just getting the water temp right."

"Well, it's going to turn hotter just because you're in it," Autumn quipped, wincing at the corny line.

"Oh. Is that so?"

"So what size tub do *you* have? One like mine?"

"Nooooo. Luxury-sized for me."

"That's it. Make me jealous."

"It has to be," Jess pointed out in her defense. "My boobs alone need plenty of room to float. And I'm not exactly a small gal either."

"I think you're just fine."

"Thanks. But you haven't really seen me outside of that picture." She pondered this. "Unless... did you check me out when we were in the closet at your party?"

Autumn spoke guiltily. "I... uh, might have peeked a

little while you were leaving."

"Naughty girl. So, you've seen me?"

"Just for a second. From the back."

"Ugh. My condolences."

"I think you're just perfect, Jess." She hesitated. "Have you seen me?"

"Well, no. I played by the rules and *kept* the blindfold on," she replied indignantly. "Unlike *some* people I could mention."

"You *sure* you didn't see me at the mall?"

"Nope. Told you, had to work."

"Or... at the... um, the hotel?" Autumn was embarrassed to even bring up the Four Seasons, given the way she'd completely melted down and fled.

"Nope." Quiet and thoughtful.

"Jess?"

"Yeah?"

"I'm... sorry about that. The hotel thing. I was just...

really nervous. And, uh, insecure."

"No apologizing. Besides. I think we made it over *that* hurdle. Don't ya think?"

Autumn replayed the events of Brenda's party in her head — specifically, Jessica fucking her in the walk-in closet. She blushed. "Yeah, I'd say so."

"Mmm. Water's just right. Hold up while I get naked."

"Stop, you're turning me on!"

A shocked gasp. "Huh. You mean you weren't already?" Jess sighed. "I'll have to step up my game."

"Oh, I'd say it's already stepped up."

There was a soft sound of splashing water as Jess eased into her bath. "Ohhhh. This feels nice."

Autumn took a sip of her drink. As usual, it was vodka. Once again, directly from the bottle.

Over the phone, there was a whirring sound, and then things got noisier.

"What's that?"

"Oh, it's probably a little loud, sorry. My tub has whirlpool jets."

"You *bitch*," exclaimed Autumn enviously.

"What? You don't have them?" Jessica's voice oozed innocence.

"No, I don't *have them*," Autumn snapped. "I live in an apartment complex owned by a cheap landlord, which means an eighty-eight dollar, plain white bathtub from the hardware store."

"Mmm, sorry to hear that, Autumn! Because one thing that's really nice about these whirlpool jets..."

"What?"

Jess didn't reply, but Autumn could hear her friend's breathing growing more labored, soon accompanied by a smattering of soft moans.

"Oh, you little *bitch!*"

"Mmmmmmm." She gasped softly. "Oh. *Right* there."

"Bitch," Autumn snarled again, although she was getting incredibly turned on by Jessica's performance.

"You know, Autumn, it's a *big* tub. Plenty of room for two."

A thrill shot through her at the very thought. "Uh..."

"And I can show you how to use the jets."

"Um, I'm sure I can figure *that* out."

"I'm sure you can." She went quiet for a few seconds. "Sorry. Sometimes I can be a little too... aggressive. I don't mean to be pushy."

"It's okay." *And whatever you do, don't stop "pushing," Jess.*

On the other end, Jessica continued to purr as the whirlpool did its work. Autumn listened, rubbing her clit in tandem with her friend's moaning. To add to the experience, she decided to give a little narration.

"I'm rubbing myself, Jessica. Thinking of... *mmm*... your fingers doing it."

"Or my tongue."

Autumn groaned.

"I want to taste you, Autumn."

"I want to... taste you too, Jess. And touch you."

Jess cried out in pleasure as she came. "Fuck yes! I'm all yours, Autumn!"

"All yours too, baby," Autumn panted, continuing to please herself.

"OHHHHHHH!" The delicious sound of Jessica's now-multiple orgasm flowed into Autumn's ear through the Bluetooth piece.

"Jess, you're so sexy... fuck..."

"You too, Autumn. Ohhhhhh! You know... you may not have... a whirlpool, but... mmm, ... you do have... a shower wand."

That, I do! Unfortunately, it involved easing herself out of the water and standing up to retrieve the shower massager from its holster. She turned the water on, lifted the stop to activate the shower, and then twisted the shower head to the *pulse* setting. Slowly, she settled herself back into the tub and eased the wand between her legs.

"You got some... action over there... now?" Jess gasped.

"*Mmm-hmm.* I'll say," murmured Autumn as she deftly directed the high-pressure pulse where it was most needed.

"Well, come on," her phone friend purred. "You've got some... ahhhhh... catching up to do."

All things considered, Autumn thought she made excellent time.

"That was wonderful, Jessica. *You're* wonderful."

"You're not so bad yourself."

They'd enjoyed their mutual "bath fun" for what had seemed like hours, lasting through several additions of hot water and Jessica's Bluetooth battery dying. Finally, they both just soaked there, talking and relaxing.

"I suppose I should be getting to bed. I've gotta work in the morning."

"Damn. That sucks." Autumn frowned. "Guess I should get out of here too. Landlord's probably going to give me some kind of notice if I keep using all the hot water."

Jess laughed. "Can he do that?"

"I don't know." Autumn shrugged. "He'd probably try though."

"Tell him you were spending quality time with your girlfriend."

"I'll do that." *Because it's the truth.*

"Well, I guess I'd better say goodnight. Now *this* phone is beeping at me. About to die."

"Okay."

"Nite, sweetie."

"Good night." She hesitated. "I love you, Jessica." Checking the phone, she saw that it was already indicating *Call Ended.*

But a few minutes later, after she'd slipped into her nightshirt and crawled into bed, her phone buzzed to indicate *(1) New Text Message.* This one was from her area code and from a local exchange.

I love you too, Autumn

Smiling from ear to ear and warm all over, Autumn

drifted off to dreamland.

She dialed, pausing before she hit the green button to place the call. In all the time she'd been talking to Jess, this was the first time Autumn was placing the call. She pressed the call button.

Four rings, and then "Hey, it's Jessica! Leave me a message! Bye now!"

Impatiently, her heart pounding, Autumn waited through the inevitable message about waiting for the tone, what she could do for more options when the message was finished, and the like.

Beep...

"Hi, Jess. Seven o'clock. 742 Evergreen Terrace. Apartment 208." Momentary nervousness and panic made her pause. For a split second, she wondered which button she was supposed to hit to erase the message and re-record it. Maybe something along the lines of *hope you're having a nice day, bye!*

But then other thoughts asserted themselves. Not least

of all, how impossibly *soft* Jessica's lips had been. *And will be.*

"I won't be wearing a blindfold this time, Jess." Deep breath. "In fact, I *might* not be wearing much of anything. *You* probably should, though." She laughed nervously. "Wouldn't want you to get arrested for public indecency."

She wondered what to say next. *If you can't come, that's cool* was her first thought. But she willed herself not to chicken out.

"See you tonight, Jessica. I can't wait." It was only as she ended the call that Autumn realized she was shaking all over.

6:55 p.m. Autumn checked herself in the mirror. She puckered her lips, making sure the neon pink gloss wouldn't smudge. All good, and it left her lips with that sultry, moist look.

Wet.

All the way from the kitchen, the zesty Italian aroma wafted in. Autumn had made spaghetti tonight —

although, if all went well, dinner could very well come *after* dessert.

She straightened the silky robe, adjusting the sash ever so slightly so the garment fell open just a little bit in the front — enough to make it obvious Autumn was naked underneath. She was feeling confident and self-assured, and realized it was because Jessica had rubbed off on her.

Nevertheless, when her phone rang, she jumped a foot in the air.

Although Jessica's phone number was no longer a matter of national security, she'd gone with *UNKNOWN CALLER* once more. In the two seconds it took her to pick up the phone and answer it, Autumn's mind raced through a gamut of dire thoughts.

She's calling to say goodbye.

She can't come tonight.

My message was too forward.

She just wants to be friends.

She's getting back with an ex.

This is the last time I'll hear from her.

"H-hello?"

"Hi, Autumn."

"Hey, Jess." Autumn was uncertain whether her heart was still beating a mile a minute — or had stopped.

"About the message you left me."

Her throat was suddenly dry. "Yes...?" she rasped.

"I spent all afternoon thinking about it."

Autumn's heart felt ready to drop, and she swore she could feel tears waiting in the wings behind her eyelids.

Say something, *dummy,* she prompted herself. "Jess..."

"When you said I should wear something, so I don't get sent to jail for public indecency."

"Yeah?"

"Well. I was going through my closet. And I just *happen* to own a trench coat."

Autumn exhaled sharply.

"You mean..."

"I'm downstairs. In your parking lot."

A grin began to form, growing wider as the world resumed existing around her. Tears did come now, but they were of excitement and joy.

"I love you," she whispered.

"You excited?"

"Yes."

"What are *you* wearing?"

"Robe."

"Oooooh. You mean?"

"Yours."

"Ours," Jess corrected, making Autumn glow all over. "Tell me what you want to do with m—"

"You're in the parking lot?" Autumn cut in. *Time to be assertive.*

"Yes. Right downstairs."

"Then stop talking. Hang up that phone. And get your sweet little ass up here."

That wonderful laugh again. "Well, okay then. I'll—" But Autumn ended the call, tossing the phone onto her table. Something told her she wouldn't be needing it for a while.

Once more, she adjusted the sash. Then, after a moment's reflection, she removed it from its loops and let it fall. The robe fell farther open, revealing even more skin and leaving very little to the imagination.

Through the door, Autumn heard the sound of footsteps on the apartment stairwell at the end of the hallway. They reached the second floor, growing louder, then slowing... and stopping in the hallway outside.

Knocking. Soft and gentle, but confident. *Like everything else about her.*

Heart pounding, shaking from head to toe with excitement, she opened the door.

As Autumn stepped forward, Jessica took two steps into the apartment, and they meshed. This time, without the constraint of blindfolds or darkness, their lips connected. Perfectly, as if meant to be. As they kissed, Jess pushed Autumn backwards, deftly shutting the door with her heel.

"Hi, Autumn," she breathed when the kiss finally broke. "It's nice to finally meet you. I'm Jessica." And once more, she sealed her lips to Autumn's.

THE END

ABOUT THE AUTHOR

I'm a longtime reader of romance, erotica, sci-fi and horror. I've aspired to become an author and have been working toward this for a few years. My first goal for 2018 was to actually make it happen, and with a few sixteen-hour days, you're holding the fruition of my dream in your hands!

Other than my sister, who is my best friend in the world, my family doesn't know I write. Manuscripts of Girl Talk and especially, Team Mom would probably not be well-received at Easter Brunch. Same holds true with the "day-job" profession I'm in—so, I keep those circles at arm's length when it comes to my writing.

When I'm not writing, I enjoy playing board and card games—the real, physical ones. Although my sister Allison and I do play Words With Friends and I even let her win a few. I also like to cook, often prompted by seeing something delicious posted on social media. I'm deathly afraid of heights and won't go near the railing at the mall, but I've actually jumped out of an airplane. So go figure.

I look forward to taking my readers on a journey

CPSIA information can be obtained
at www.ICGtesting.com
Printed in the USA
LVHW010940230821
695886LV00002B/123

9 781985 852815